I've never felt this way before about anyone. I guess I really am in love. I just hope this doesn't mean I turn into some gushy, servile idiot—like Nina, for instance.

Oh . . . maybe that's a little harsh. I am happy for Nina — and Benjamin, too, for that matter. For a long time I was jealous of them, because I never thought I'd experience that closeness or compatibility with anyone myself. I never thought I'd find someone so perfectly tailor-made for me — until I met Aaron.

The only problem is that Aaron's mother is marrying my father.

Don't miss any of the books in
Making Out
by Katherine Applegate
from Avon Flare

Coming Soon

Avon Books are available at special quantity discounts for bulk purchases for sales promotions, premiums, fund raising or educational use. Special books, or book excerpts, can also be created to fit specific needs.

For details write or telephone the office of the Director of Special Markets, Avon Books, Inc., Dept. FP, 1350 Avenue of the Americas, New York, New York 10019, 1-800-238-0658.

MAKING OUT #12

Claire, can't lose

KATHERINE APPLEGATE

AN AVON FLARE BOOK

AVON BOOKS, INC.
1350 Avenue of the Americas
New York, New York 10019

Copyright © 1996 by Daniel Weiss Associates, Inc., and
Katherine Applegate
Published by arrangement with Daniel Weiss Associates, Inc.
Library of Congress Catalog Card Number: 98-93667
ISBN: 0-380-80868-4
www.avonbooks.com/chathamisland

First Avon Flare Printing: April 1999

AVON FLARE TRADEMARK REG. U.S. PAT. OFF. AND IN OTHER COUNTRIES, MARCA REGISTRADA, HECHO EN U.S.A.

Printed in the U.S.A.

WCD 10 9 8 7 6 5 4 3

Zoey

Am I worried about the future? What a question. I guess everybody worries about the future at this time of year. The closer people get to January first, the more they say ridiculously corny things like, "This next year is going to be my year—I can feel it."

Of course, at this time last year I probably said something just as corny myself. And as the current state of affairs clearly demonstrates, this year was not "my year."

It's almost funny. Almost. I mean, thinking about my life a year ago is almost like thinking about a different person. First of all, college still seemed impossibly far

1

off, so I didn't have to worry about applications, recommendations, or the possibility of never seeing my friends again after the summer.

I was also head over heels in love with Jake McRoyan. At that point, he was the only boyfriend I'd ever had—and the only one I'd ever wanted to have. Lucas Cabial (who may or may not ~~be~~ my current boyfriend) was still locked up in Youth Authority. And I'd never even <u>heard</u> of Aaron Mendel.

In other words, life wasn't hopelessly confusing.

But my life isn't the only one that has changed beyond recognition. Who would have thought back then that Benjamin and Claire would break up? Or that Benjamin

2

would start dating Nina? Or that Nina would have lost her virginity by the end of the year...or, for that matter, that Aisha would be almost engaged?

Whew. It's a little mind-boggling. In a way, all the changes that have taken place this year make me even more nervous about what's ahead. I suppose worrying about the future inevitably involves a lot of thinking about the past. And I guess that's also why New Year's Day is a time when people try to forgive and forget.

I don't know about anyone else, but speaking personally, forgiving and forgetting are not high on my list of priorities right now.

I'm tired of forgiving people. I mean, I forgave my parents for cheating on each other. I forgave them for inviting Lara McAvoy, my obnoxious and possibly alcoholic half sister, to come live with us. I forgave Benjamin for not telling me about his operation right away. I even forgave Lucas for cheating on me with Claire....

Oh, yes—I've tried to forgive myself, too.

That's the hardest part. If only I could turn back the clock and take back all the times I kissed Aaron or talked to him or even thought about him, I think my outlook on the future would be a lot more positive. But if there's one thing I've learned this year, it's that you can't undo the past.

So, in answer to the question—yes, I'm worried about the future. Probably more worried than I've ever been in my entire life.

One

After a long and virtually sleepless night, Zoey Passmore finally decided to pull herself out of bed.

She sat up straight and leaned against the pillows for a moment, staring out her dormered window at the gray Maine sky. It looked like another cold, bitter, colorless day. *Another lousy morning,* Zoey thought dismally. Even on Christmas—when she'd had her first (and, she hoped, her last) hangover—she had felt better than she did right at that moment.

She glanced at the clock by her bed. It was almost ten. She couldn't hide in her bed all day. She had to be at the restaurant by eleven at the latest, and after what had happened the night before, she couldn't afford to be late.

As if on cue, the front door slammed and footsteps slowly padded up the stairs. Zoey's jaw tightened. *Lara.*

The footsteps paused outside her room, and there was a tentative knock on the door.

"Go away," Zoey snapped hoarsely.

"Zoey, please," Lara pleaded. "I just want to explain—"

"Explain?" Zoey interrupted. "Explain why after

you nearly burned down my parents' restaurant, you ran straight for my boyfriend's house?''

"Zoey, come on, I—"

"Or maybe you just want to explain why you didn't even bother to help clean up," Zoey cut in. "Do you know that Christopher and I were in that kitchen for almost five hours last night?" Her voice rose. "What were you *thinking*, Lara?"

"I went over to Lucas's to get some advice, Zoey—I swear.''

"Advice?'' Zoey couldn't help laughing. "What—you wanted him to help you brush up on your making-out skills?''

"I didn't even kiss him!" Lara shouted. "I'm not even interested in him! Look, I screwed up last night with the restaurant, okay? I admit it. But I didn't go over to Lucas's house to make out with him. The *last* thing I want is for you to think that anything is going on between Lucas and me. I like Jake, remember?''

As if that's supposed to make me feel better. Even though Zoey held no romantic feelings for Jake anymore, she couldn't help feeling a mild pang of resentment whenever she thought of Lara and Jake together. What could Jake possibly see in her? He had enough problems of his own without having to deal with some nut case.

"Zoey?'' Lara asked after a moment.

Tossing the covers aside with a swift, violent motion, Zoey stormed across the room and threw open the door. Her face instantly wrinkled in disgust. Lara was standing before her in her tattered polka-dot pajamas, with her dirty-blond hair bedraggled and her vacant, puffy blue eyes fixed to the floor. The faint, sour odor of alcohol hung in the air.

"Have you been drinking?'' Zoey cried in disbelief.

6

Lara shifted on her feet. "I had a few sips of tequila when I got home last night," she muttered. "I was feeling—"

"Was this before or after you paid Lucas a visit?" Zoey hissed.

"I told you, I wasn't there to fool around with him." Lara looked up. "I was there because I felt bad about the fire, and I thought Lucas would know how to cheer you up."

"That's—that's—" Zoey sputtered, but she was too infuriated to continue. Did Lara actually think Zoey would buy that lie? Well, maybe she did—after all, she was probably drunk. Zoey brushed past her and marched straight for the bathroom, slamming the door loudly.

"I'm sorry, okay?" Lara yelled. "I don't know how many times I can say it!"

Zoey took a deep breath and closed her eyes. "Let me put it to you this way, Lara," she said. Her voice was shaking. "No matter how many times you say it, it's not gonna be enough. *Saying* anything won't solve our problems. But getting off your lazy, ugly, hung-over butt right now and going down to my parents' restaurant will. How's that?"

There was a pause. "Well," Lara said spitefully, "I'll just get off my lazy, ugly, hung-over butt, then." Zoey could hear her stomping down the stairs, and a moment later the front door slammed shut.

"And clean yourself up!" Zoey screamed.

Suddenly she realized that tears were streaming down her cheeks.

She wasn't even crying so much over the fact that Lucas had cheated on her *again*—unless Lara was telling the truth, which was about as likely as the temperature on Chatham Island suddenly rising to a balmy sixty-five degrees. No, at that moment she was crying far more because *she*, Zoey Passmore, had been reduced to taking cheap shots, such as calling people "ugly." She'd never done that before in her whole life.

What's happening to me?

Sniffing, she stepped over to the sink and took a peek in the mirror. Her face, though drawn from lack of sleep and red from crying, was still recognizable. She still had the same blue eyes and same tousled dark blond hair. She couldn't have changed *that* much in the past few weeks, could she?

"You're a pathetic little brat," Lara had said to her the previous night at the restaurant. "Perfect little Zoey, everybody's darling. You've got everybody believing you're an angel. But you are far from an angel. You don't even deserve a guy like Lucas. . . ."

Luckily, Lara's little speech had ended right there. Of course, that had been because they'd realized that Lara had accidentally set the kitchen on fire.

Zoey turned the faucet and waited for a moment for the water to get hot. Maybe Lara was right. Maybe Zoey *didn't* deserve Lucas. Lara was definitely right about Zoey's being far from an angel—although she doubted if she was still "everybody's darling." After all, everyone knew about Aaron.

I've become everything I promised myself I never would be, she said to herself. *A lying, cheating, unfaithful—*

The phone started ringing.

Zoey quickly dashed out of the bathroom and down the stairs. It was probably Lucas, calling to explain himself. She bolted around the corner into the kitchen, her bare feet slapping on the floor. There was always a chance she *had* been wrong about the events of the night before. . . .

8

"Hello?" she answered breathlessly.

"Hi, Zo, it's me," said her father. "I'm just calling to let you know that Benjamin is out of surgery and in the recovery room care."

For a moment Zoey was unable to speak. A sickening wave of emotions swept over her, dominated primarily by guilt, then worry. She'd completely forgotten that her own brother had been scheduled to undergo surgery that morning—surgery that could very possibly change the rest of his life.

"Zoey?" her father asked.

"Is—is he all right?" she finally managed.

"Well, according to Dr. Martin, everything went smoothly," Mr. Passmore said, obviously making a concerted effort to sound as cheerful as possible. "But we won't know the results for a week or so. Benjamin's eyes are bandaged, and it will take at least that long for them to heal."

Zoey swallowed. "So . . ."

"So the doctors are optimistic," Mr. Passmore said. "Other than that, I can't really say."

"I see. How . . . how is he?"

"I haven't had a chance to talk to him yet. He's still unconscious." He hesitated. "Look, Zo—I know it's hard, but try not to worry, okay? He already made it through the toughest part."

"Right," Zoey said, but the word was empty.

Mr. Passmore cleared his throat. "So how's the restaurant? Are you and Lara managing okay?"

Zoey swallowed again. "Just fine," she said. It would probably be best *not* to tell her father about the fire. He had enough on his mind for the moment—and besides, there had been no permanent damage.

"Is Lara there?" he asked. "Can I speak to her?"

"She's in her room getting dressed," Zoey answered quickly.

"Well . . . okay," he said. "Just tell her that Benjamin is fine. Nina and your mother are with him right now. They send their love."

Zoey just nodded. Tears were welling up in her eyes again. "I—I think I'd better go," she choked out.

"Don't worry, Zo," her father soothed. "Everything's gonna work out fine."

"I know," she mumbled. "Bye, Dad."

Zoey clumsily hung up the phone. She stared at the wall for a moment, then burst into another fit of convulsive sobs.

Why couldn't I have just gone with them? she repeated to herself, slumping down at the kitchen table. Poor Benjamin was lying unconscious in some strange hospital bed, not even knowing whether he would see again, and she was trapped on the island, alone. She stared across the frozen backyard at Lucas's house. Burning anger filled the pit of her stomach. If she had gone with her family and Nina to Boston, she wouldn't have even seen Lara and Lucas together. None of this would have happened. . . .

Gradually Zoey stopped crying. She'd had enough misery in her life over the past few months to know better than to think *what if*. And as much as she tried to convince herself that she was desperately upset over Benjamin, she knew it wasn't true. Deep down, she knew that she felt the way she did because she had probably lost Lucas forever.

Lucas Cabral sat on the edge of his bed in only a pair of boxers and a T-shirt, staring at the wallet Zoey had given him the night before. Well, not *given*, exactly. She'd thrown it at his head.

For the first time since he'd been locked up in Youth Authority, he hadn't slept. Back then, of course, he'd had insomnia for a specific reason—namely because he was worried some deranged skinhead punk might suddenly try to put a knife in his back. That kind of sleeplessness was acceptable. But tossing and turning all night over a girlfriend—no, an ex-girlfriend—was not.

He couldn't believe that Zoey had called him a bastard. True, he had called her a bitch once, but that was only after she had used that word to describe herself. He hadn't even called her a bitch when he'd walked in on her making out with Aaron Mendel.

He angrily ran his hands through his long, disheveled blond hair. Thinking about it now, he realized he definitely *should* have called her a bitch when he'd caught them together. Or a slut. After all, she had called Lara a slut the previous night—and compared to Zoey, Lara was a model of morality.

Still, even after that scene, he hadn't been able to resist opening the neatly wrapped Christmas present. And when he'd seen the wallet, with his initials embossed in gold on the shiny black leather, he'd almost felt like forgiving her. *Almost.*

Lucas laughed out loud. How hypocritical could Zoey get? It wasn't as if Lara had been in his room with all the lights off, moaning passionately, with her shirt unbuttoned and her tongue crammed down Lucas's throat. And that was precisely how he'd found Zoey with Aaron.

He tossed the wallet aside and began pacing around the floor. Maybe he *should* have made a move on Lara. She had been giving him signals, hadn't she? At this point, he figured, he might as well go ahead and get his kicks any way he could. What better way to get back at Zoey than following up on Lara's little surprise

11

visit? Maybe he'd give the newest addition to the Passmore family a call that very morning.

A car pulled into the driveway, and a minute later the doorbell rang. Lucas frowned.

"Lucas?" his father called in his thick Portuguese accent. "Are you awake?"

"Yeah. What is it?"

"There's somebody here to see you," Mr. Cabral answered gruffly. Lucas heard some muted conversation, then his father added in a confused voice, "Christopher Shupe?"

Lucas rolled his eyes. What was Christopher doing there at ten-thirty in the morning? That kid had a serious knack for bad timing. "Send him up," he said reluctantly.

Heavy footsteps pounded up the stairs, and a second later there was a knock on the door.

"Come in, Christopher," Lucas mumbled, sitting back down on the bed.

"What's up, dude?" Christopher asked, stepping into the room and pulling off his hat and gloves. "I didn't wake you up or anything, did I?"

"Nope." Lucas shook his head. "I haven't slept."

Christopher paused. "Are you all right?" He frowned, peering at Lucas closely. "You don't look so hot."

"No, I guess I'm not all right." Lucas yawned, then put his face in his hands. "But enough about me," he said sarcastically. "What brings you here so bright and early?"

"Look, maybe I should just come back—"

"No, no, it's all right," Lucas said. He jerked his head toward his desk chair. "Have a seat. You coming from Eesh's?"

Christopher nodded, then flopped down at the desk.

"Yeah—I was just having breakfast up there." He shrugged. "I . . . uh . . . thought I'd stop by before I had to be at the restaurant."

Lucas grunted.

"Zoey troubles again?" Christopher asked hesitantly.

" 'Troubles' doesn't even come close to describing it."

"Is she . . . uh, is she mad about what happened Christmas Eve?"

Lucas shot him an angry look. "Is *she* mad?" he snapped.

Christopher blinked a few times. Then an apologetic little smile appeared on his lips. "Look, Lucas, I think I'd better be on my way. . . ."

"No, no—stick around. I'm just a little worn out." In spite of everything, Lucas felt himself smiling as well. "I shouldn't get mad. I guess I *did* get a little out of hand on Christmas Eve."

Christopher laughed. "You did what anyone else would have done. But it's a good thing Zoey and Claire stepped in. I heard you were *mad*. You probably would have floored that guy."

"Yeah, I probably would have." Lucas shuddered, thinking about how concerned Zoey had looked when he grabbed Aaron in the hall. He knew that face of hers well. She'd been wearing the exact same expression on the day, many months earlier, when Jake had tried to pick a fight with Lucas. It had been on the ferry, when everyone still thought Lucas had killed Jake's brother, Wade. And she'd stepped in to stop Jake, just as she'd done with him.

Lucas's stomach twisted painfully. That had been the first indication that Zoey was falling for him. It seemed like a lifetime ago.

". . . besides, it wasn't as if you were the only one who caused a scene," Christopher was saying. "You should have seen Zoey after you left. She got completely tanked."

"Huh?" Lucas asked, not quite believing what he had just heard. "Zoey got drunk?"

"*Drunk* is a serious understatement." Christopher's expression soured. "She was singing Whitney Houston songs and telling me I was about to become *Mr.* Aisha Gray."

Lucas couldn't help laughing. "Wow. Sounds pretty crazy. Maybe I should have stuck around."

"Believe me, it wasn't pretty."

"Well, you know what they say about booze," Lucas said with a needling grin. "It brings out everyone's secrets. I mean, you *are* gonna be Mr. Aisha Gray, aren't you?"

"Very funny."

"What's the deal between you guys, anyway?"

Christopher sighed. "I really don't know, man," he said, shaking his head. "I guess that's why I'm here."

"Yeah," Lucas muttered, "I had a sneaking suspicion you weren't here to console me about my relationship with Zoey."

"I just can't take the waiting," Christopher went on. "She told me she was going to give me her decision New Year's Eve. That's Tuesday night—and today's only Friday."

"It's not all that far off," Lucas offered lamely. Under the circumstances, it was the best he could muster. He wasn't exactly in the most sympathetic mood.

"Maybe not," Christopher replied. "But it's torture. I mean, there I was, having breakfast with the whole family just now, and I had to pretend everything was normal. Eesh hasn't even *told* her parents yet. She was just smiling and laughing, as if nothing had changed. I thought I was gonna lose it.''

"Well, at least you're still going to family breakfasts," Lucas said. "That's a good sign, isn't it?"

Christopher shook his head, looking around the room agitatedly. "I don't even know anymore, man. Maybe she's just humoring me before I ship out."

"When *do* you ship out?"

"The fifth. A week from Sunday."

Lucas nodded. He swallowed, suddenly feeling strangely empty. For the first time since Christopher had told him the news about his plans to join the army, Lucas realized that Christopher was actually leaving Chatham Island—for good. It was weird. In a way, Christopher had become his best friend. There wasn't really another guy he could even talk to. Benjamin was in his own bizarre world with Nina, and Jake was, well, *Jake*.

"What's up?" Christopher asked.

"Nothing, nothing," Lucas said distractedly. He walked over to his closet and grabbed a pair of jeans. "So let me guess," he said. "You thought that since I'm so tight with Zoey, and Zoey's so tight with Eesh, I might be able to pump Zoey for a little information?" He slipped into the pants. "Trying once again to prove your theory about the old Chatham Island network?"

Christopher raised his right hand. "Guilty as charged." He flashed a wicked smile. "Damn, Cabral—I guess you know me pretty well."

Lucas cocked an eyebrow. "What, because I know that you're low enough to use your friends to find out your girlfriend's secrets? It doesn't take a genius to figure that one out."

"Yeah, I guess not." Christopher looked at him hopefully. "So what do you think? Zoey's gotta know *something,* right? Can you help me out?''

"I would if I could. But I don't think I'm gonna be talking to Zoey anytime soon." *And now that you're leaving, I really don't think I'll have a reason to talk to her anymore.* Lucas shook his head. He realized something else about Christopher then, too: In a way, Christopher was the last connection he had to any kind of life on the island. It was pathetic.

"Come on," Christopher snorted, oblivious to Lucas's sudden silence. "You guys always make up."

Lucas sank back down on the bed. "Past tense, man," he said, no longer able to keep from sounding as depressed as he felt. "We *used* to always make up. But I think last night was the straw that broke the camel's back."

"Why?" Christopher's eyes narrowed. "What happened last night?"

Lucas bit his lip. "Ah . . . Zoey walked in on Lara and me."

"What?" Christopher yelled.

"Nothing was going on," Lucas said hastily, waving his hands. "She was worried about Zoey. She came over because—"

"She felt bad about nearly burning down the Passmores' restaurant?" Christopher finished. "Yeah, I know all about it. I spent the whole evening with Zoey cleaning it up. Let me tell you something, man—that girl Lara is bad news."

Lucas sighed. "Yeah. I kinda figured."

Christopher glanced at the clock by Lucas's bed. "Speaking of the restaurant, I'd better get going." He stood and put on his hat and gloves. "We're supposed to open at noon, and the kitchen is still kind of a mess."

"Sorry I can't be of more help," Lucas mumbled.

16

Christopher paused at the door. "Don't sweat it." He smiled. "Anyway, I'm sure you guys will make up by tonight, which means that by tomorrow I'll have all the information I need. If there's one thing I learned about Chatham Island, it's that it's very predictable."

"I wouldn't count on it," Lucas called after him. "I really think it's over between Zoey and me." He listened to Christopher start down the stairs. How could he feel so sorry for himself? Maybe it was all for the best that he and Zoey had broken up. Maybe he just needed to close a few chapters in his life and start over fresh.

"Hey, Christopher?" he called.

"Yeah?"

"If you want to know what Zoey knows, maybe you should go ask Aaron Mendel."

Two

"I don't get it, Claire," **Aaron** said for about the tenth time in a row. "I mean, why? Why did you come over here if you didn't even want to . . ."

"Have sex?" she finished harshly.

He didn't reply.

Claire sat up in Aaron's bed. She tossed a few strands of long, lustrous black hair out of her eyes and fixed him with an icy glare. "Is that all you think about, Aaron?"

Aaron groaned and rolled over, turning away from her. Claire had to admit that even from behind he was gorgeous. His shoulder muscles rippled as he pulled the covers over his back.

"Well, yes, it's what I think about when a beautiful girl slips into bed with me in the middle of the night," he said finally. "Is that wrong?"

"It's wrong if I'm not the person you really want to have sex with," Claire replied evenly.

Aaron twisted to face her again, his hazel eyes blazing. "What do you want from me, Claire?" he barked. "Just tell me, okay? I'm a little confused right now."

Claire didn't answer right away. The truth of the matter was that she wanted *him* to want *her*—but there was no way she was going to tell him that. Besides, he would end up wanting her sooner or later. She was sure of it.

"I only want you to be happy," she said finally. And that was true. She *did* want him to be happy—but she knew he would be happiest with her, not Zoey. The only problem was making him realize it.

"You have a funny way of showing it," he muttered. "Do you really think that leading me on will make me happy?"

"How was I leading you on?" she asked, feigning surprise. "I wanted to *kiss* you, Aaron. It's not my fault that you wanted more."

He turned over again and gave her a sly, sexy smile. "Well, I do want more," he breathed.

Claire felt her heartbeat accelerate, and she was instantly disgusted with herself. Since when had something as stupid as a smile ever had such an effect on her?

"I'm sorry to disappoint you," she stated. She tossed the covers aside and sat on the edge of the four-poster bed, bending down to pick up her shoes. Her fingers trembled as she pulled them on. It was time to leave this cozy little room at Aisha's parents' bed-and-breakfast. She had long overstayed her welcome. "I think I'd better be going."

"No—wait," Aaron said. She felt his hand brush the back of her shirt, sending tingles up her spine. "You're right. I was being . . . hasty."

Claire shook her head, then stood and whirled to face him. "You're just saying that, Aaron. I *know* you. Better than you think."

He raised his eyebrows. "Do you, Claire?" he asked smugly.

Claire frowned. For a brief moment she was tempted

19

to bring up Julia—the girl who had written to him over the summer, the girl who had wondered why he hadn't kept in touch. Claire had found her letter a few weeks before, when she'd decided to do a little investigating. But bringing *that* up would be unforgivably stupid. Not only would he get angry and defensive, but he would also know that she had been snooping around his room.

"I know you want Zoey," she said finally.

He laughed once. "Yeah, it's pretty clear you know that. That's why you told Lucas Cabral I was visiting her the other night." His tone grew harsh. "That's why he conveniently walked in on us and started this whole mess."

Claire shrugged, but an idea was dawning on her. Maybe she would just pretend she wasn't interested anymore. If Aaron thought that she had lost her desire after what had happened the previous night, he would finally see what he was missing. Men *always* wanted what they couldn't have. He knew Zoey liked him; that was conquered ground. Maybe Claire could make him see that it was time for him to move on.

"As I said before," she said slowly, "until very recently I thought that Zoey belonged with Lucas."

He looked at her questioningly. "You don't any-more?"

"Maybe you two belong together after all."

Aaron took a deep breath. "Why the sudden change of heart?"

She grinned as carelessly as she could. "Come on, Aaron. It's pretty obvious *we're* not meant to be to-gether."

Aaron laughed again, but the sound was brittle. "Why do you say that, Claire?"

"Well, for one thing, the way matters are going be-tween your mom and my dad, we'll probably end up becoming brother and sister," she said. "That *would* make things a little awkward, wouldn't it?"

"Oh, I don't know." Aaron propped himself up in bed. "One big happy family . . ."

"Very funny," Claire snapped, avoiding looking at his perfectly defined chest, which was now plainly visible. "Anyway, I don't believe in sleeping together on the first date. Maybe not even the tenth."

He sneered. "Was last night your idea of a date?"

"No. But I'm definitely *not* ready to sleep with you."

He sighed ruefully. "Yeah. Well, that's one thing you and Zoey have in common."

Claire's eyes widened. "You haven't tried—"

"No, no," he mumbled, shifting awkwardly in bed. "It's just that, uh . . ."

"It's just *what*, Aaron?" she demanded.

"She doesn't know I want to have sex with her," he said under his breath.

Claire clucked her tongue. "I find *that* one seriously hard to believe."

"Why, Claire?" Aaron snapped. "What's so hard to believe about that?"

"Because that's not like you, Aaron," she said with a smirk. "You tend to come on strong."

He shook his head, rubbing his eyes with his palms. "Yeah, well, I guess you *do* know me pretty well."

"So?" she prodded.

"So what?"

"So why haven't you told her you want to have sex with her?" she asked crossly.

"I don't know if that's any of your business, *Claire*," he shot back.

"Fine." She turned, grabbed her coat off the back of his chair, and walked toward the door. "I'll just be on my way. But if you want my advice, don't play games with Zoey. Tell her what's on your mind. Be honest. Because if there's one thing that girl can't stand, it's dishonesty."

Claire slammed the door behind her, feeling momentarily triumphant.

Then she froze.

In her haste, she'd forgotten where she was. She was in the guest wing of Gray House. And she had just made a very loud noise. This was not a good idea for someone who had sneaked in the night before and was supposed to be at the other end of North Harbor.

Aisha Gray's ears perked up at the sound of a door slamming somewhere in the guest wing of the B&B, then the sound of feet pattering quickly down the hall. Aaron must have finally woken up. Judging by the urgency of his footsteps, he was probably racing out to meet Zoey somewhere.

Aisha leaped out of bed—where she had been lying ever since Christopher left, staring at his ring and feeling generally miserable—in order to intercept Aaron in the hall. This was a perfect opportunity to take her mind off her own depression. If Aaron had just woken up, he was probably hungry. She would offer to make him breakfast. And in doing so, maybe she would get to the bottom of what was going on between him and Zoey.

"Hey, Aaron, I was—" She broke off when she saw the figure on the stairs.

It wasn't Aaron.

It was Claire.

Aisha's jaw dropped.

For the briefest moment Claire hesitated—then she hurried down the rest of the steps. "Hey, Eesh," she sang out in a strained, unnatural voice. "I was just upstairs saying hi to Aaron."

Aisha stared as Claire rushed past her and headed straight through the foyer for the door. She couldn't believe her eyes. What was Claire doing there? And she looked absolutely horrible. Her flawless white skin was pasty, she had bags under her eyes, and her long black hair was a tangled mess. Her clothes were rumpled, as if she had slept in them. . . .

"Bye, Eesh," Claire called when she reached the front door. Her face looked slightly pinkish now. "Sorry, I can't talk—I'm running a little late."

"I—I didn't hear you come in," Aisha finally stammered.

"I guess I must have been quiet," Claire answered. The front door slammed behind her.

Aisha stood very still for a moment, unable to do anything but gape at the door. What had *that* been all about? Claire had definitely not just come in to say hi. There was no way anyone could climb those stairs without Aisha's noticing; her room was right next to the stairwell. That meant Claire must have come in earlier—maybe while Aisha had been eating breakfast with Christopher.

Or maybe Claire had come in much earlier than that.

Aisha's nose wrinkled in a mixture of bewilderment and revulsion. Claire and Aaron? After everything that had happened at the party the other night? There had to be an explanation; that scenario was just too ludicrous. After all, their parents were practically engaged. . . .

Suddenly she felt as if the bottom had just dropped out of her stomach.

She was practically engaged, too. *Practically*. And

in another five days—a mere 120 hours—she had to decide whether she was or she wasn't.

Sighing heavily, Aisha walked through the foyer and into the living room. She peered out the window down Climbing Way, hoping to catch another glimpse of Claire, but the elder Geiger sister was already long gone. Aisha shook her head. Compared to her friends, she was actually pretty lucky when it came to romantic entanglements.

Very lucky, the more she thought about it. Zoey and Lucas and Claire and Aaron were involved in some twisted love triangle—or square, or quadrangle, or whatever. And poor Nina, the only other girl on the island with a stable relationship, was currently in Boston, worrying if her boyfriend would ever see again.

But Aisha didn't have any of those problems. She was head over heels in love. She couldn't even conceive of being with anyone else. And her boyfriend was perfectly healthy. In fact, he was a flawless specimen of manhood.

So why didn't she feel lucky?

Nina

What, me worry about the future? No way, Jose. I know that my future will be great. It'll be just like Brenda Walsh's future on <u>Beverly Hills 90210</u>. The character was canned years ago, but according to the show, she's off in England becoming a famous stage actress or something.

That's kind of how I see my life progressing.

Seriously, what could I possibly worry about? Okay, so my boyfriend is getting a dangerous operation, which might not even work. Maybe he'll never regain his sight. Or maybe he will be able to

See again—in which case he'll run off with a girl who doesn't look like me. (I look like a cross between Edward Scissorhands and a large female hog.)

No, losing Benjamin doesn't worry me. As I said, sooner or later I'll end up like Brenda Walsh—maybe starring as the Cowardly Lion in a zany British version of The Wizard of Oz on Ice. And why would Benjamin Passmore mean anything to me at that point?

I guess I could also worry about Zoey (the other Passmore sibling and my best friend) going off to college, meeting new and exciting people, and forgetting about me entirely. Benjamin, too, for that matter.

But there's nothing I can do about that. Besides, you have to take the good with the bad. After all, my sister, Claire, will be leaving Chatham Island as well. That means I'll be able to crank my stereo as loud as I want, and I'll never have to think twice about disturbing Claire's coven meetings or animal sacrifices.

Of course, I could always worry about my father marrying a dwarf named Sarah Mendel....

There's no point in going on. Biting sarcasm and delusional escape fantasies are the way I cope with my worries. I'm not very well adjusted.

Three

"Nina, are you sure you don't want to come back to the hotel with us?" Mr. Passmore asked. "Dr. Martin said it might be as long as three hours before he wakes up."

Nina shook her head. "I, uh, I just want to see him," she said. "I don't mind if he's not awake."

"Are you sure?" Mrs. Passmore asked. "These waiting rooms are so unpleasant."

Mr. and Mrs. Passmore were both hovering over her. They were doing a very good job of adding to her anxiety—which at that moment was already threatening to send her into cardiac arrest.

Nina managed a smile. "No, thanks." She took a deep breath. "Look—no offense or anything, but . . . I just kind of . . ."

"Wanted to be alone," Mr. Passmore finished understandingly. "No offense taken, Nina." He reached into his back pocket and pulled out his wallet, then fished out a couple of crumpled bills. "Here's some money in case you get hungry. We'll see you in a bit."

Mrs. Passmore bent down and kissed Nina on the top of the head. "Good-bye, dear."

Nina clutched the money and watched as Mr. and

Mrs. Passmore headed for the elevator, Mr. Passmore with his gray ponytail bobbing up and down and Mrs. Passmore with her dark blond hair tucked up under a wool hat. How could they be so nice and so cool at the same time? All the other parents she knew seemed to have given up their coolness a long time ago. The perfect example, of course, was her father—who upon meeting Sarah Mendel had been transformed into a human version of Barney the Dinosaur.

Nina sighed and shoved the bills into her pants pocket. She definitely would not use the money for any more food. She'd already had two candy bars that morning.

No wonder Mr. Passmore thought I'd get hungry, Nina thought miserably. She studied the small roll of flesh that protruded from under her flannel shirt and hung over the waistband of her black jeans. *He was probably worried I'd go berserk and try to break into one of the snack machines.*

Her gaze swept across the little waiting room. Luckily there were no vending machines nearby. Well, that wasn't quite true. There *was* a vending machine—but it didn't sell food. No, that was quite clear from the sign above it: If You're Not Ready to Use Condoms, You're Not Ready to Have Sex.

Nina blushed.

The last time she'd been alone in that hospital waiting room, she'd ended up having the most embarrassing experience of her entire life.

Even now, the memory of how Dr. Martin had caught her lurking in front of the condom dispenser made her cringe. She recalled every word of his little speech: "If you two have indeed made the decision to become sexually active, you must make sure that Benjamin follows the instructions for applying the condom exactly as given on the packet.''

She shook her head. She still couldn't believe he'd actually *said* that. The guy was about as romantic as a fence post. Still, thanks to him, she and Benjamin had gone on to consummate their relationship—and safely, at that. Besides, Dr. Martin had probably known exactly what he was doing. Doctors were smart.

The thought was reassuring. Dr. Martin *was* smart; he was one of the most gifted, capable doctors at Boston General. Benjamin was lucky to have him as his surgeon.

Nina was beginning to feel hopeful—in spite of the horrible fluorescent lights, the foul odor of cafeteria food, and the fact that Benjamin was still unconscious. So far, everything had gone according to Dr. Martin's plan. Benjamin had been the perfect candidate for the surgery, and he had survived. The biggest hurdle had been successfully cleared. The operation *had* to work.

Without thinking, Nina reached into her pocket and grabbed her pack of Lucky Strikes. Unfortunately, in doing so, she also happened to catch another glimpse of her paunch. She shoved an unlit cigarette into her mouth. She needed some serious work.

If Benjamin got his bandages off in a week, that meant she had to stop eating—period. And exercise maybe eight hours a day. And wash her hair, and wipe the perpetual purple lipstick off her face, and clean her fingernails. Plastic surgery and liposuction wouldn't hurt, either. One week was enough time to rebuild herself, wasn't it? After all, Tommy Lasorda had lost ten pounds in one week on the Ultra Slim-Fast diet, and that guy was a serious porker. Nina Geiger could do the same.

''Nina?'' a deep, familiar voice asked.

Nina glanced up. Dr. Martin was standing in front of the double doors to the recovery room. He looked tired and sweaty, but he gave her a weary smile. A surgical mask was still dangling from his neck.

"You can come see Benjamin if you want," he said. "But you have to put out that cigarette. There's no smoking anywhere in this hospital."

Nina decided it would be best not to explain her habit of "smoking" unlit cigarettes. "Is he . . . ?" She let the question hang.

"He's still asleep," Dr. Martin replied. "But it looks as if he may be waking up sooner than we expected. I thought you might like to be with him when he does."

All at once Nina's heart began thumping painfully. She nodded and threw her cigarette in the garbage. The operation was over—so why was she so nervous? She forced herself to stand and follow Dr. Martin through the doors.

"He's a strong patient," Dr. Martin said, leading Nina down a narrow little hall flanked by a series of plain white doors, all marked Post-op.

I know he is, Nina thought. *So there's no reason to feel as if I'm about to pass out.*

Dr. Martin paused in front of a door near the end of the hall. "Here we are. There are a couple of things you should be aware of. Benjamin may experience some discomfort when he wakes up. He'll also be disoriented."

Nina nodded, swallowing. "So you're saying I shouldn't yell 'Surprise!' " she managed.

Dr. Martin chuckled. "Exactly." He opened the door.

For a moment Nina was frozen by the ghastly sight before her. Benjamin was lying on a narrow bed, completely covered by a tight blanket except for his head and his left arm, the latter of which was connected to three dangling IV tubes. His head was swathed in a wide bandage that covered his eyes and most of his nose. What she could see of his face was very pale.

No wonder she'd been so nervous. Unconsciously, she'd been expecting to see something exactly like this.

Nina's eyes moistened. Benjamin didn't look like a strong patient. He looked like someone who had just suffered a horrible accident.

A nurse stood next to his bed, monitoring a screen that had a bunch of computerized blips running across it, all blinking and beeping at different times. She turned and smiled at Nina. "His vital signs are getting stronger," she said. "I think he'll be waking up any minute now."

Nina nodded, wondering how anyone could possibly smile in a place like that. She felt Dr. Martin's hand at her back, gently guiding her into the room.

"We're all very hopeful, Nina," Dr. Martin said. "With the exception of a few very minor difficulties, it was a textbook procedure."

Nina kept her eyes pinned to Benjamin's face. "A few very minor difficulties?" she asked. What did that mean? Didn't doctors always say that if the prognosis looked bad?

"Just some technical things," Dr. Martin soothed. "I'd explain it to you, but you might need a couple of years of medical school first."

"But it's nothing to worry about, right?" she muttered, unable to keep from sounding mildly desperate.

"As I told Benjamin's father, we'll know the results in a week."

Nina squeezed her eyes shut for a moment. That didn't exactly sound like a ringing endorsement for not worrying. It sounded more like a way of avoiding the issue altogether.

"We're hopeful, Nina," he repeated.

"Okay," she breathed. She opened her eyes again. Benjamin's fingers twitched—just barely.

"I think he's waking up now," the nurse whispered. Nina nodded. And then she burst into tears.

The first thing Benjamin noticed was a dull ache behind his eyes. He was aware that it was painful, but the pain was somehow removed, detached. It was as if he were experiencing the sensation through layers and layers of thick, cottony blackness—a fuzzy wall that separated him from reality.

Where was he?

He had no recollection of anything before this moment. His mind was absolutely blank.

But gradually, very gradually, the fuzzy layers began to peel away.

The pain in his eyes grew sharper. He also became aware of sounds—monotonous, rhythmic beeps. There was something else, too: sniffling. Somebody near him was crying.

And then he remembered.

I must have just had the surgery.

So why was he still shrouded in darkness?

He tried to blink and found he couldn't. Panic began to set in. There was an intense pressure on his eyes. The beeps around him grew louder, faster. He was still blind. . . .

"Relax, Benjamin." Dr. Martin's rumbling voice floated above him. "Your eyes are bandaged."

Benjamin tried to ask why, but all that came out was a pathetic, breathy gasp. His mouth and throat were bone dry. He couldn't even swallow. He ran his tongue over his cracked lips in a vain effort to moisten them.

"Easy there," Dr. Martin said. "Don't try to talk just yet. You've just had the operation."

The pain in his eyes had suddenly become almost unbearable. What was happening to him? Why did it hurt so much? A confused whimper escaped his mouth.

"The discomfort will subside in a few hours, Benjamin. Just take it easy."

Easy for you to say, Benjamin thought, still struggling to fully grasp what was going on. He squirmed, but for some reason he could hardly move. He tried to focus on the beeps, as if they would offer some answer. They were coming very rapidly. Sobs continued to fill the air.

"Who's . . . ?" he mouthed. "Who's . . . ?" Benjamin shook his head in frustration. He couldn't seem to form complete sentences. "Who's crying?" he finally wheezed.

A trembling hand squeezed his fingers. "It's me."

"Nina," he murmured. Warm relief surged through him, alleviating some of the pain and confusion. He held her hand as tightly as he could. "Why are you . . . ?"

"Crying?" She laughed once, then sniffed loudly. "I stubbed my toe on the way in."

"Stubbed . . . ?" Benjamin asked uncomprehendingly. He must have still been disoriented. Nina's answer didn't make any sense.

"Shhh," Nina whispered. "Don't try to talk."

Benjamin's mouth moved slightly to protest, but after a moment he decided to take Nina's advice. Talking was too much of an effort. He was far too tired and weak to do anything but hold Nina's hand.

"Pulse is rising, hovering around one-oh-eight," a woman muttered.

"Nina," Dr. Martin said, "I think you'd better wait outside."

Nina's grip on Benjamin's fingers tightened. "Why?" she asked. "Is there some—"

"We just need to give Benjamin a little time to wake up," Dr. Martin interrupted in a low voice. "Okay?"

Benjamin shook his head. "No," he mouthed silently. "Nina . . ."

But her fingers had already slipped out of his hand, and her footsteps were fading away.

"I'll be right outside, Benjamin," she called in a strained voice. "I'll be—"

A door closed, cutting her off.

"I'm sorry, Benjamin," Dr. Martin said. "It's just that we don't want to get you too excited right now. Some time alone will give you a chance to recover a little bit."

Some time alone? Benjamin wondered. He didn't want to be alone. He wanted Nina. There must have been some kind of problem. Why was Dr. Martin torturing him like this?

"Please try to relax," Dr. Martin said.

Even in the face of the sharp pain, the inability to move, and the piercing beeps filling the air, Benjamin would have probably managed to relax, if only just a little bit. But Nina's abrupt departure struck an ominous chord deep within him, something he didn't quite understand.

All he knew was that he was very, very afraid.

JAKE

Am I worried about the future? Scared is more like it. I'm scared of waking up in the morning. I'm scared of seeing a beer in the refrigerator or a bottle of tequila under Lara's bed because maybe I won't be able to resist having a drink. So yeah, the future terrifies me.

Maybe I'm also scared because of what happened to my brother, Wade. Drinking cost him his life. For a while I blamed Lucas for the accident. After all, he took the rap for it. But I know now that I was just looking for a scapegoat. Wade was responsible for his own death. And I know that if I don't clean up my act, I'll be walking in his footsteps. I'm not sure if it will take a day, a week, or even a year—I just know I won't have a future.

I guess that right now I just have to take one step at a time. I have to live day by day. But every day sober is another step into the future, right?

Four

Jake McRoyan squirmed in the metal folding chair, gazing despondently at the bare tile floor. Never in his entire life had he felt so completely wrung out. It was as if his whole body had been transformed into an old, dry washcloth. He had a terrible pounding in his head—but that was probably from the injury he had sustained when his stereo came crashing down on top of him the night before.

"Look, Dad," he mumbled, "maybe we should come back another time. I'm feeling kind of—"

"Out of the question," Mr. McRoyan stated firmly.

Jake groaned and leaned back in his chair.

He and his father had been the first to arrive—and so far they were still the only people in the room. Jake knew the room well. It was a classroom at Weymouth High School, but the desks had been cleared out and about a dozen folding chairs had been placed in a circle in the middle of the floor. Until that morning, when his dad had dragged him off the ferry and led him there, Jake had had no idea that the school was also used for Alcoholics Anonymous meetings.

"Are you sure this is the right place?" Jake asked, gingerly rubbing the Band-Aid that covered the gash in his forehead. The wound hurt far more that morning than it had the night before—but that wasn't a huge surprise. After all, he'd been anesthetized by an entire bottle of vodka.

"Positive," Mr. McRoyan said, staring straight ahead.

Jake sighed. He still couldn't believe he had actually agreed to come there—to get on the ferry in the miserable, freezing cold and endure the nauseating ride to Weymouth. He couldn't believe he had actually gotten out of bed. "But wasn't the meeting supposed to start—"

"Try not to be so antsy, all right?" Mr. McRoyan interrupted. "These meetings never start on time."

For some reason—even in his lamentable condition—the comment struck Jake as funny. *Of course they never start on time,* he thought with an ironic grin. *Everybody's hung over.*

His father turned to look at him. "Why are you smiling?" he demanded sharply. "Do you think this is some kind of joke?"

Jake's grin abruptly faded. "No, sir," he murmured, averting his eyes. After what had happened, he knew that this was no joke.

Mr. McRoyan had found Jake on the floor, completely and utterly bombed, with his stereo lying next to him. Jake had been trying to reach the volume knob, but he'd misjudged the distance and had knocked the whole thing down on top of himself. But probably the worst part of his father's discovery was that Jake hadn't even been drinking with anyone. He had been drinking alone.

Not since Wade's death had Jake seen his father so emotionally devastated. But the pain and shame of the night had definitely had one positive effect: Jake would never drink again, *ever*. He couldn't let his family down anymore—or himself, for that matter. He suddenly regretted even having suggested leaving. Any suffering he endured now was worth it.

The door opened, and three men shuffled into the room. They smiled awkwardly at Jake and his dad, then took seats in the circle. None of them sat next to each other.

Jake stole a few quick glances at the new arrivals. They all looked to be around Mr. McRoyan's age or older, but it was hard to tell. Their faces were haggard and etched with deep lines, particularly around the eyes, giving them all a gaunt, skeletonlike appearance. Jake shivered involuntarily. They didn't look like guys who liked to knock back a couple of cold ones every now and then. They looked more like people who were suffering from some horrible, debilitating disease.

Alcoholism is *a disease*, Jake reminded himself, repeating the words his father had said to him that morning. Would Jake himself end up looking like those men if he didn't stop? Probably not, he realized. He'd probably be dead long before he reached their age.

The door opened again, but Jake kept his eyes pinned to the floor. It was too depressing to look. . . .

"Jake?" a familiar female voice asked. "Is that you?"

Jake's head jerked up. The mild queasiness he'd been feeling all morning suddenly increased to severe nausea, wrenching his stomach violently.

Louise Kronenberger was standing in front him.

"Louise?" he gasped, then shut his mouth for fear of vomiting.

"I'm happy to see you here," she said with an easygoing smile. For once in her life, she wasn't wearing an outrageously tight dress or low-cut shirt—just a

41

sweater and jeans. Her long, curly brown hair was pulled up in a bun. "I could use a friend."

Jake was speechless. *A friend?* This was K-Berger, Weymouth High's number-one party girl—the very same girl who had seduced him one night in a wild binge of booze and cocaine and stolen his virginity.

"I'm Mr. McRoyan," Jake's father said, extending his hand.

Louise took his hand and shook it vigorously. "Louise Kronenberger," she said. She sat on the other side of Jake. "I know Jake from school."

"I gathered that," Mr. McRoyan said. He gave Jake a puzzled glance. "Are you all right, son?"

Jake managed a nod. *Fine*, he thought wretchedly. *Louise just forgot to add that she knows me in the biblical sense, too.*

"So, are you and Jake in the same grade, Louise?" Mr. McRoyan asked.

Louise nodded.

"And how long have you been coming to these meetings?"

"I started about a month ago," she said. Her smile grew wistful. "I, uh, guess I just kinda reached the end of my rope. This is my fourth time here."

Mr. McRoyan nodded gravely. "Good for you."

The piercing nausea that had briefly immobilized Jake was slowly beginning to subside, leaving a confused numbness in its place. The situation was almost surreal. If someone had told him a day earlier that within twenty-four hours he'd be sitting in an AA meeting in a classroom, sandwiched between his father and K-Berger, he most likely would have laughed hysterically—or punched that person in the face.

"Is this your first time, Jake?" Louise asked tentatively.

He nodded, still afraid to open his mouth.

"And it won't be his last," Mr. McRoyan stated. "Now that he has a friend here, he'll be even more inclined to come. You can keep an eye on him for me."

"I'd be happy to," she said.

I'm sure you would, Jake thought grimly. If there was one thing Louise Kronenberger was good at, it was keeping an eye on the boys of Weymouth High. Jake glanced at her, then at his father. He suddenly felt as if he were in a really bad cartoon, with a cartoon angel on one shoulder and a cartoon demon on the other.

"He can keep an eye on me, too," she added. "I need all the support I can get."

"Yeah, right," Jake muttered.

"I can understand if you're angry," she said, shrugging. "People need space. Sometimes the past hurts too much."

Jake stared at her confusedly. At first, in his tired, sickened state, he had just assumed that every word out of her mouth would be a lie; her entire life revolved around lies. But something in her tone touched him. She actually sounded sincere. And her face looked different—softer, less probing, less manipulative. For the first time since he'd met her, she didn't look as if she was either on the prowl for sex or zeroing in for a kill.

"It gets easier, though, Jake," she murmured. "Trust me."

Maybe she was right, Jake reflected. After all, if he could believe Louise Kronenberger, *anything* was possible.

Five

Zoey decided that she would not stop by Lara's room on her way out to see if her half sister had already left. Zoey figured that at this point they needed as much time apart as they could manage—especially considering that they had to spend the next ten hours together. A little solitude before work would be good for both of them.

The frigid winter air whipped at Zoey's face as she slammed the front door and headed down Camden to South Street. She tucked her head into her scarf and moved quickly, dreading the prospect of having to put on a smile and play hostess all day. Fridays were always pretty busy, even in winter. And Lara's mess had yet to be entirely cleaned up.

Zoey frowned. Any regrets she'd had about insulting Lara earlier had faded. The truth of the matter was that Zoey couldn't think about her without getting furious. But fury wasn't necessarily a bad emotion. It kept her focused. And it kept her mind off Benjamin.

The wind picked up when Zoey turned left onto South Street, blowing directly at her from across the harbor. She hunched over, staring at her feet as they moved across the cobblestones. Why did she have to live in a place that was so bitterly cold? Why couldn't she live in Florida or Hawaii or the Virgin Island?

Then again, she *would* be moving someplace warm if she got into any of the colleges she wanted to attend. In less than nine months she'd be on her way to college in California: Stanford or Berkeley or UCLA. The thought of it suddenly filled her with an intense longing, coupled with nervousness. She'd done well that semester, but she had to get cracking on her applications. As soon as she got home that night, she would start her essays.

She turned right on Dock Street, surveying the ferry landing and the dark line of the mainland beyond. There had been a time in her life—not too long before—when she'd thought she had everything she would ever need right there on Chatham Island. She'd loved everything about it: its isolation from the mainland, its quaint houses with their shingled roofs, the lighthouse on the islet . . . and above all, the cobblestoned streets of North Harbor, along which she and all her dearest friends lived. The mere thought of leaving for college had been enough to terrify her.

Now it seemed as if she were counting the days until her departure.

Maybe I'll meet somebody at college, she thought dreamily. After all, most people met their future spouses at college, didn't they? She could imagine herself falling in love with some dark, tall southern California native, somebody who would make her forget all about Lucas Cabral and Aaron Mendel. Somebody sweet and intelligent, who wouldn't lie or cheat on her, who shared her passion for writing and her sense of romance. . . .

Zoey forced her wishful thoughts aside and ducked into the little alley behind her parents' restaurant. She

45

nearly slammed into Christopher's new car.

New wasn't quite the word. She paused for a minute, staring at the rusted, dented pile of junk. Most island residents kept their good cars over on the mainland, using older cars to get around the island, but if Chatham Island ever had a contest for best island car, this would definitely take first prize. Why Aisha had given it to Christopher was still a mystery. He was leaving for good in a little over a week. Maybe Aisha had secretly been hoping that owning a car would somehow convince Christopher to stay.

Shaking her head, Zoey sidestepped the car and walked to the kitchen entrance. *Everybody here is going crazy.*

Christopher threw the door open after two knocks and grinned. He already had his apron on. Without even pausing to say hello, he waved his hands around the tiny stainless-steel kitchen area. "So what do you think?" he asked proudly.

Zoey looked around, amazed. Every surface had been wiped clean. It looked as if Lara's disaster had never happened. "Wow," she said. "Thanks a lot, Christopher. How'd you do it so fast?"

"It was nothing. Just remember, if you're in a jam, I'm your man."

"I think I *will* remember that," she muttered. "You seem to be the only man in my life who comes through for me." She hung up her coat, then peered out the swinging door to the main part of the restaurant. "Did Lara help you?"

"Nah. She's not here yet."

Zoey made a face. "Figures."

Christopher looked at her curiously. "I thought you guys would have come together. You know, being as you live in the same house and all."

"Yeah, well, things are a little tense between us right now," she grumbled.

Christopher just nodded. He opened his mouth as if he were about to say something, then bit his lip.

"What?" Zoey demanded.

"Nothing, nothing." Christopher shook his head, then opened the refrigerator and began laying vegetables out on the table.

"Christopher, I am *not* in the mood to play guessing games right now," Zoey snapped. "If you have something to say, say it."

He took a deep breath. "Lucas would kill me," he mumbled.

Zoey's face darkened. "I may kill him first. What did he say?"

Christopher looked at her apprehensively. "Nothing happened between him and Lara last night, you know."

Rage instantly engulfed her. "No, I don't know that. How do *you* know? Were you there?"

"Lucas told me," he replied simply. "He wouldn't lie about something like that to me."

"Give me a break," she spat. "Like I'm supposed to believe that?"

"Believe what you want, Zoey." Christopher's tone was deliberately calm and measured. "But that's the truth. And you don't need to yell at me. I can hear you just fine."

Zoey paused for a moment. What was her problem? For about the fifth time already that day, she had lost control of herself. It wasn't only embarrassing, it was frightening. She stared at her feet in the awkward silence. Christopher began washing lettuce.

"I'm sorry," she said finally. "I didn't mean to get angry with you."

Christopher just shrugged. "It's cool. You're upset."

"No, it's not cool," Zoey said. "You're just trying to be a good friend to Lucas. And to me."

"Oh, I don't know about that," Christopher said with a doubtful laugh. "He may think a little differently on the subject."

"So when did you talk to him?"

"Right before I came here." Christopher tossed the lettuce into a colander and began washing tomatoes. "I was going to ask him to pump you for a little information." He laughed again ruefully. "Looks like I picked the wrong time."

Zoey wrinkled her brow. "A little information?"

Christopher paused and looked at her. "Yeah, about a certain friend of yours. You know, the one I want to marry?" He rinsed another tomato under the faucet.

"Oh, jeez." Zoey put her face in her hands. "Christopher, I am so sorry. . . ."

"Uh-oh. I don't like the sound of that."

Zoey looked up at him again. "No, no—it's just that I've been so wrapped up in myself and my own stupid problems that I totally forgot about what's going on with you and Eesh. Well, not *totally*." She shook her head. "Look, believe me, whatever *is* going on is just between you two. Eesh won't tell me a thing."

Christopher snickered. "Why do I find that so hard to believe?"

"It's *true*, Christopher." Zoey managed a smile. "This is one issue I definitely want to avoid. Whatever you guys decide is your business and your business alone."

"Is this really coming from Zoey Passmore—the starting link in the Chatham Island gossip chain?" Christopher teased.

"Hey, I'm not as bad as some people," Zoey argued, grinning. "Look at Nina. And look at *you*. I mean, thanks to Christopher Shupe, everyone on Chatham Island ended up finding out about Benjamin's operation before me."

Their smiles faded at the same time.

Christopher turned off the faucet and began slicing the tomatoes on the counter. "Have you heard anything about that?" he asked after a moment.

"Yeah," she said. Her voice was strained. "My dad called about an hour ago. I guess everything went fine, but we still won't know for another week. Benjamin's eyes need to heal, so he won't get his bandages off until then."

He nodded gravely. "Well, when you talk to him, tell him good luck for me, all right?"

"I will," Zoey breathed. A deep affection for Christopher suddenly flowed through her. She hadn't realized just how much she'd grown to like him. In the past, she'd tended to think of him as a childish, self-centered kid who used his good looks to get what he wanted—namely, as many girls as possible. But even if that had been true when he first arrived, he'd grown up so much. He was a loyal friend, an amazingly thoughtful boyfriend (once he'd made up his mind to be faithful), and one of the few people on Chatham Island who could actually admit to a mistake.

She wished she could say something equally as nice for herself.

"You know, Christopher," she began, "I hope everything works out between—"

A loud pounding on the door interrupted her.

Christopher raised his eyebrows. "You-know-who," he mouthed.

Grimacing, Zoey walked to the door and opened it.

Lara stood before her, her face blank. Zoey's eyes flashed over Lara's outfit. She was wearing a tight little cutoff T-shirt that showed her belly button and a very tight pair of blue jeans—totally inappropriate attire for a waitress.

"Well, are you gonna let me in?" Lara demanded, chomping loudly on a piece of gum. She pulled her jacket around her. "I'm freezing."

Zoey stepped aside. "Yeah, well, maybe if you'd *worn* a little more, you'd be warmer." She slammed the door behind them.

"What?" Lara asked. She blinked a few times. "You got a problem with what I'm wearing? Is it too *ugly* for you, Zoey?"

Zoey clenched her fists, fighting to retain her composure. "It's not *ugly*," she breathed. "It's just not something a waitress should wear."

"Oh, yeah?" Lara looked over Zoey's shoulder at Christopher. "What do you think, man?"

He didn't look up. "It's not something I've ever seen Zoey or her mom wear," he muttered, staring at the pile of sliced tomatoes in front of him.

Lara shrugged. "Well, Dad never said anything to me about a dress code. It's not my fault." She took off her coat and tossed it onto the counter, barely missing the tomatoes. "I guess you'll just have to deal with it."

"Or you'll have to go home and change," Zoey replied evenly.

"You would do that to me, wouldn't you?" Lara leaned forward unsteadily, as if she had lost her balance. Her gum snapped loudly in Zoey's face. Suddenly Zoey noticed another odor besides spearmint.

"You're *drunk*!" Zoey cried, horrified.

"I am *not*." Lara rolled her eyes. "I had a Bloody

Mary before I came here. You know, just to take the edge off. Big deal.''

''I see,'' Zoey said hollowly. She shoved Lara aside and threw the door open again. An icy blast of wind filled the kitchen. ''Get the hell out of here. Now.''

Lara just giggled. ''Zoey, you are ridiculous. Look at yourself right now.'' She glanced at Christopher. ''Come on, man, tell Zoey how ridiculous she's being.''

Very calmly, Christopher picked up Lara's coat and tossed it to her. ''My name's not 'man,' '' he said quietly. ''It's Christopher. And Zoey isn't the one who's being ridiculous.''

'' 'My name's not *man*,' '' she repeated. ''Well, *man*, I don't give a crap what your name is.'' She pulled on her jacket and marched out the door. ''I didn't want to work today anyway.''

Zoey slammed the door. She spun around and looked at Christopher, her eyes wide with fury.

Christopher just stared at her.

For a moment the kitchen was absolutely still.

Then a smile broke on Christopher's face.

Before Zoey knew what was happening, the two of them were howling with laughter.

Zoey felt as if a dam inside her had just broken wide open. Only once before in her life—about three weeks earlier, when she had seen Jake outside her house with a bottle of tequila—had she felt that life had reached a point of absurdity beyond comprehension. But in retrospect, this moment was far worse. She needed to grip the sides of the counter to keep from falling over.

''Ohhhh boy,'' she said when they had finally gained control of themselves. ''Just another boring day in North Harbor, huh, man?''

''You know it, man.'' Christopher shook his head,

then pointed at the clock on the wall. It was already eleven forty-five. "And we've got exactly fifteen minutes to find a substitute waitress."

Claire was just drifting off to sleep when she heard the phone ring. *Please let it be for someone else*, she silently prayed.

"Claire?" she heard her dad call from all the way down on the first floor. "Phone for you, dear."

Claire groaned and rolled over. "Can you take a message, Dad?" she shouted back. "I'm really, really tired."

There was a pause, and then her father shouted, "It's Zoey, Claire. She says it's an emergency."

Claire was instantly awake. An emergency? That could mean only one of two things—that Aaron had called Zoey about the previous night's rendezvous or that Aisha had called Zoey about finding Claire in the B&B that morning. Both possibilities were unacceptable. She grabbed the phone off her nightstand.

"Got it, Dad," she breathed. She waited for him to hang up on the other end, then asked, "What's up, Zoey?"

"You're not gonna believe this," Zoey mumbled.

Claire swallowed. She would have to think fast if she wanted to have any hope of defending herself. "Believe what?" she asked.

"Lara showed up for work drunk this morning."

Claire frowned. For a moment she felt like saying, "So what?" "Wow," she finally got out, trying unsuccessfully to sound outraged. "That's pretty lousy."

"*Lousy* is an understatement. I threw her out of the restaurant—but now I have a little problem." Zoey hesitated. "I, ah . . . I need a waitress."

Claire smiled, feeling very, very relieved. So *that*

was the emergency. If Zoey had known about the events of the night before, she definitely would *not* be asking Claire to come down to Passmores' and lend a hand.

"Claire?" Zoey prodded. "Are you still there?"

"So you're offering me a job?" Claire asked.

"Just for today, Claire," Zoey begged. "Come on—you know I don't ask you for favors that often."

Claire smirked. That was quite true. Zoey hardly ever talked to Claire these days if it wasn't absolutely necessary. "Well, I don't know, Zo . . . I really wanted to work on my college applications today. . . ."

"*Please.* Look, it's not like I'm asking you to do it for free. You'll make some money. I would ask Eesh, but what with the situation between her and Christopher right now, it might get a little awkward—"

"I'll do it," Claire said hastily. Asking Eesh was not an option. Claire *had* to get to Zoey before either Eesh or Aaron did. And this little favor would be the perfect opportunity.

"Thank you so much, Claire. I owe you one."

Claire almost felt like saying the same thing. "It's no big deal, Zoey. So, when do you want me there?"

"As soon as possible."

"I'll grab my coat."

"Thanks again." Zoey hung up the phone.

Claire grinned again as she hung up and placed her own phone back on the nightstand. *Waitressing*, she thought with a laugh. That was one job she'd never thought she'd have. But fate and luck worked in mysterious ways.

BENJAMIN

If someone had asked me in August if I was worried about the future, I would have honestly replied no. The future was very clear to me at that point. I would finish my senior year as Benjamin Passmore, the mysterious blind wonder, and then go off to college to become—once again—Benjamin Passmore, the mysterious blind wonder.

Now I have no idea who or where I'll be.

It may sound a little ridiculous, but before the operation, I always thought I'd end up a music critic. It made perfect sense. I'd be able to go to any concert for free, and then I'd dictate to my assistant insightful, droll bits about what I'd heard. A blind music critic would be pretty marketable, right? I think I would be unique. I can just imagine the ads: "Benjamin Passmore: He can't see—so his ears are extra trustworthy."

Now, a formerly blind music critic might be a little more difficult to sell.

I guess being blind makes you focus on the present a little more than a sighted person would. Getting through a day is difficult enough when you're scared to cross an unfamiliar street.

Of course, if I regain my vision, I'll have that burden of fear lifted from my shoulders. Sure, I won't be unique—but I won't be handicapped, either. I'll be just like everyone else.

And that worries me a little bit, too.

But what worries me most is the immediate future. If I don't regain my vision, I'll be the same person I've been for the past seven years. But I've already had that glimmer of hope. I've already begun making plans. I already have expectations.

If the surgery fails, I'll lose those hopes and plans and expectations forever.

Six

By the time the pain and grogginess had finally lifted, Benjamin found that he was hungry. Several hours must have passed; Nina and his parents had returned, and the three of them were crowded around his bed, jabbering away nervously in an effort to keep the atmosphere light. The noise was beginning to get on his nerves.

"Is there anything you want me to tell Zoey when we call, dear?" Mrs. Passmore asked.

"Yeah," Benjamin mumbled. "Tell her to express-mail several large pepperoni pizzas to the hospital."

Mr. Passmore laughed. "Hey, you've gotten your appetite back. That's probably a good sign."

"Maybe I can smuggle in some candy bars," Nina whispered, running her hand through his hair.

The door opened. "Hello again, everyone," Dr. Martin said warmly. "How are you feeling, Benjamin?"

"Hungry," Benjamin replied.

"Healthy teenage boys are *always* hungry," Dr. Martin remarked. "We'll get you some food in a minute. I was actually wondering about your eyes."

Benjamin swallowed. "Well, they feel a lot better now than when I first woke up."

"Good, good," Dr. Martin said, somewhat distractedly. "Excuse me, Nina. I just want to check out a few things right now."

Feet shuffled; Benjamin was aware of Nina stepping back and Dr. Martin moving forward to lean over him. He felt some pressure on his eyes through the bandage.

"How does that feel?" Dr. Martin asked.

"Uh . . . okay," he said doubtfully. It didn't exactly hurt—but it didn't feel so great, either.

"How about this?"

The pressure shifted, and a searing pain instantly stabbed through Benjamin's forehead. "Ow!" he cried.

Dr. Martin took his hands away, and the pain receded. "Hmmm," he murmured. "That hurt a little, huh?"

"A little," Benjamin admitted, suddenly feeling very frightened and vulnerable.

"Well, that's all for now." Dr. Martin took a deep breath and moved away. "I'll see what I can do about getting you a late lunch, okay?"

"Dr. Martin?" Benjamin asked tentatively.

"Yes?"

"What just—I mean, uh, why did it hurt just now? Is there anything I should—"

"You're going to feel some tenderness for the next few days, son," he explained.

But for the first time Benjamin seemed to notice a hint of warning and finality in the doctor's tone, as if he were saying, "Don't pursue that line of questioning any further."

"Do you have any other concerns?" Dr. Martin asked.

"Uh . . . no," Benjamin answered. But he was lying. "Tenderness" was not excruciating pain. Then again, if Dr. Martin were really worried about something, he wouldn't be leaving the room. . . .

"Hey, Benjamin, I think I'll walk out with Dr. Martin," Mr. Passmore said. "I'm going to give Zoey and Lara a call at the restaurant. I'll see if I can rustle up some chow on the way back, okay?"

"Yeah, fine." Benjamin sighed. "Tell them I said hello."

"Me too," Mrs. Passmore added.

"Me three," Nina chimed in.

The door closed. For several seconds the room was quiet, except for the steady beeps of the machines monitoring his vital signs.

"Are you all right?" Nina asked quietly, placing her hand on top of his.

"Never better," Benjamin mumbled.

"Just hang tough, kiddo," his mother encouraged. "You're doing fine. Nobody said this was gonna be easy."

He laughed. "Yeah," he said flatly. "I guess you're right about that."

"Hey, you know what?" Nina said, suddenly sounding full of excitement. "Dr. Martin told me that your hospital room has free HBO."

Benjamin frowned. "Uh, Nina? I can't *see*, remember?"

"Who cares about you? I was thinking about me."

A smile glimmered on Benjamin's fact. Leave it to Nina to say the perfect thing at the perfect time. He squeezed her hand tightly. "That's good. You'll have an incentive to come visit."

"Well, now you know the *real* reason I wanted to stay here with you for a few days," she said. "It's not every day we Geigers get free access to premium cable channels."

"I don't know if your father would approve of all that television," Mrs. Passmore said in a mock stern voice. "It's a good thing I'm here to chaperone you."

"Oh, *man*," Nina whined. "Does that mean we'll have to drink sparkling cider on New Year's Eve?"

"Not *we*, Nina," she said. "You and Benjamin. Jeff and I have our own plans," she added slyly.

"Uh-oh," Benjamin said. "We all know what that means: getting out your old beads, putting on the Jefferson Airplane, and reminiscing about the glory days while you suck down margaritas."

"Very funny, wise guy." Mrs. Passmore slapped his arm playfully. "You kids are just jealous because you missed out."

"Missed out on bell-bottoms and words like groovy?" Benjamin snickered. "I feel so deprived."

"Is that what you guys really do on New Year's Eve?" Nina exclaimed. "That is so cool. I wish my father had been a hippie."

"Nina," Mrs. Passmore said, "we were *not* hippies—"

The door suddenly crashed open.

"What is it?" Mrs. Passmore asked, sounding alarmed.

"I just spoke to Zoey," Mr. Passmore said. His tone was brisk.

Benjamin bit his lip. Warning bells were going off in his brain. "Uh, that was a pretty short conversation," he said.

"Yeah, well, apparently there wasn't a whole lot to talk about. Lara showed up drunk for work this morning. Claire is filling in for her."

Mrs. Passmore gasped.

"Oh, jeez," Benjamin mumbled. "What happened?"

"Zoey said that she was cursing and staggering," he said hopelessly. "I guess Zoey and Christopher threw her out of the restaurant. Claire was nice enough to agree to sub for her."

Claire subbing? Probably not without some ulterior motive, Benjamin thought, but it was not the time to start wondering about any of Claire's schemes. "What are you gonna do?" he asked.

"I don't know," Mr. Passmore replied in a low voice. Benjamin could hear him pacing. "I feel like I should go up there," he muttered under his breath.

"What does Zoey think?" Benjamin asked matter-of-factly.

"She wants me to stay with you. She says she'll be able to manage. I want to stay, too, but . . ."

"But leaving Lara and Zoey alone together in that house is *not* a good idea," Benjamin finished. "Believe me, Dad, I will not be offended if you go home." He smiled weakly. "The sooner the better, if you ask me."

"I'll be here with Benjamin," Nina volunteered, stroking his hand. "He'll be fine."

"Benjamin's right, Jeff," Mrs. Passmore said. Her voice was grim. "*One* of us has to go up there and deal with this situation."

The hunger that had been tugging at Benjamin's stomach was gone. It was amazing how domestic strife could kill an appetite. So the seemingly perfect reconciliation between his mother and father was still a little tenuous. There was nothing like a major catastrophe involving his father's illegitimate daughter to remind everyone that all was not well within the new Passmore family.

Finally Mr. Passmore sighed. "I'll get the early bus tomorrow. It'll put me in Weymouth at around ten-thirty."

Silence filled the room once again.

"What are you going to do, Dad?" Benjamin asked after a moment.

"I don't know," he said. "But whatever it is, I'm gonna make damn sure that this never, ever happens again."

Seven

The moment the four o'clock ferry docked at Chatham Island, Jake leaped off onto solid ground. It was amazing just how good solid ground could feel. For a while out there on the bay, Jake had seriously thought he was going to puke all over the deck.

Luckily, his father had to take care of some business in Weymouth; he wasn't going to get home until nine-thirty. Jake needed some time alone. He was still in a daze. The AA meeting had lasted about three hours—and it would probably take at least twice as long for him to process all the stories he'd heard. His father was right; it had been very educational. *Shocking* was a better word for it. Compared to some of those people—including Louise Kronenberger—Jake was as sober as a priest.

He glanced at Passmores' as he walked across Dock Street. Lara would be there now, helping out. Maybe he should stop by and say hello. She'd been on his mind more than once in that stuffy little classroom. Maybe he could even hint—in a careful way, of course—that she could follow his example. If anyone could benefit from an AA meeting, it was Lara McAvoy.

Summoning his resolve, he marched up to the door of the restaurant and pushed it open. His jaw immediately dropped.

Claire was there.

She was wearing a little waitress's apron over a very sexy jumper. She was also smiling at a table full of males—all of whom looked to be in their mid-twenties—and thanking them for their generous tip.

Jake blinked. *Claire Geiger* was thanking people for a tip.

"Jake!" Zoey called, waving at him from behind the cash register. "Hey—c'mere!"

Claire turned around and winked at him slyly as he walked toward Zoey. What was going on? He didn't get it. Was this some kind of elaborate practical joke?

"How's it going?" Zoey asked.

Jake shrugged. "I'm a little confused," he said, unable to tear his eyes away from Claire. "What's *she* doing here?"

"You don't know?" Zoey asked.

Jake turned to look at her. She seemed to be eyeing him with a strange intensity. "No," he said slowly. "Should I?"

"So you haven't talked to Lara today?"

"Actually, that's why I'm here," he said. "Is she in the kitchen or something?"

"I don't know where she is," Zoey stated.

Jake shook his head. He still felt as if it had been used as a punching bag the night before. Nothing was making any sense. "You're going to have to start over, Zoey," he moaned. "It's been kind of a long day."

"Don't tell me you were drinking last night, too."

"What?" Jake's jaw tightened. "Who said I was?"

Zoey's eyes grew soft. "Nobody did," she murmured. "Look, I'm sorry. It's just that Lara came in to work drunk this morning. I told her to get lost. That's why Claire is here."

"*Claire* agreed to fill in for Lara?" he asked, flabbergasted. He cast a furtive glance over his shoulder to make sure she hadn't heard. She was still laughing with her customers as they gathered their coats. She'd obviously made a big hit with them. "Did you bribe her or something?" he asked.

Zoey just shook her head sadly. "You know what the pathetic thing is, Jake?"

His eyes narrowed. "What?"

"That it's much more surprising to you that Claire did me a favor than that Lara was bombed at eleven this morning."

Jake chewed his lip for a moment, feeling like a complete and utter fool. But he couldn't argue with her. "You're right," he said finally. "It *is* pathetic."

Zoey twisted her lips into a forgiving little smile. "Needless to say, I'm not in the greatest mood. You got any suggestions about what I should do with Lara?"

He shrugged. "You haven't talked to her since this morning?"

"I don't even know where she is. I was kind of hoping you would."

She's probably passed out on her bed right now, Jake thought—but he kept the hunch to himself. "I'll look around," he said vaguely. "Look, I'd better go."

"Give me a call if you find her," Zoey called after him.

Jake didn't reply. He kept his head down as he trailed the last of the fawning stragglers from Claire's table out the door. Zoey obviously meant that he should give her a call *when* he found Lara. In her subtle way, Zoey had given him a mission that he couldn't turn down. He had to hand it to her—she was good at that.

The only problem was that hunting down Lara McAvoy had suddenly become the last mission on earth he wanted to get involved with.

"So did Jake come in to offer an excuse for Lara?" Claire asked once the door was shut and the restaurant was completely empty again.

"No," Zoey replied. "He hasn't seen her all day. He said he'd call when he found her."

Claire raised her eyebrows. "You aren't *concerned* about her, are you? She was the one who royally screwed you over."

"Yes and no," Zoey mumbled. "I mean, I just don't want her to do anything stupid before my dad gets home."

Claire nodded understandingly. She realized for the first time that day just how serious this crisis was for the Passmores. Benjamin was lying in some strange hospital bed—in considerable pain, from what she understood—and Mr. Passmore had to leave him to deal with some idiot child who could possibly destroy his business. A momentary pang of guilt shot through her. That *should* have been why she had agreed to help out in the first place—but it wasn't.

"Look, Claire," Zoey said, forcing a smile. "I know you're sick of hearing this, but I really, really appreciate your helping me today. You don't know how much it means."

Claire laughed. "I'm not sick of hearing it. Besides, I kind of like waitressing." It was true. So far she'd only had to wait on four tables, and they'd all given her enormous tips. It was actually pretty fun. Her feelings of guilt began to subside. So what if she had shown up for a self-serving reason? In this case, the ends definitely justified the means. She was helping a friend; there was no denying that.

"You know, Claire," Zoey continued cautiously, "I really want us to be friends."

"We *are* friends, Zoey."

"I know, I know," she said quickly. "It's just that sometimes . . ." She hesitated.

"Sometimes you think my sister should be committed to an insane asylum?" Claire suggested dryly. "Don't feel bad about that, Zoey. I've felt the same way for years."

Zoey laughed. "No . . . I mean, yes, sometimes I do think that." Her expression grew serious. "It's just that . . . sometimes things aren't straight between us."

Claire stiffened.

"And I don't want that to happen anymore," Zoey stumbled on. "You know, between any of us on the island. Time is getting short. We aren't gonna be here forever. I mean, graduation is only six months away."

"I wouldn't worry about it too much," Claire said dismissively. She wasn't about to get emotional with Zoey and match her confession for confession; too much was at stake with Aaron. Besides, she meant what she'd said: She truly valued Zoey's friendship. At the same time, she was well aware that she was using Zoey at that very moment for her own purposes. But friendship was a complex and many-sided thing. Nobody knew that better than Claire.

"You don't think about what's going to happen to us when we all pack up for college in September—and leave each other for good?" Zoey asked.

"Right now I'm thinking a lot more about finishing my applications so I can get into college."

Zoey nodded. "Yeah, me too, I guess. But I'm always changing my mind. I mean, this morning I was thinking that I couldn't wait to get off Chatham Island and never come back. Then five minutes later I felt like I was gonna cry because I'll miss it so much."

"You're a romantic, Zoey," Claire said, but her tone was gentle. "Believe me, getting off this island and meeting new people will be a good thing for all of us. We'll *always* be friends. If anything, the time apart will make us closer."

"Maybe you're right," Zoey replied doubtfully.

"I know I am. Besides," she added with her wintry smile, "there are only a limited number of guys here. Think about it. Pretty soon we're going to run out of options."

"Ugh." Zoey put her face in her hands and laughed. "Don't talk about it. I think we already have."

Claire laughed along with her, but part of her was thinking, *Maybe you have run out of options, Zoey, but I think I still have one left. And his name is—*

Before she could finish her thought, the door opened, and Aaron Mendel walked into Passmores'.

Eight

"Aaron!" Zoey exclaimed shrilly. Her voice sounded as if she'd just inhaled helium from a balloon. She immediately blushed.

"Hey, Zoey," he said. His tone, by contrast, was relaxed and easygoing. If he noticed her embarrassment, he pretended not to. He looked at Claire and flashed her a strange smile. "Hello, Claire. What are you doing here?"

"Working," she said shortly. Her icy black eyes seemed to be staring through Aaron, not at him.

Zoey swallowed. Why was Claire looking at him that way? Well, it probably could have been the way he looked—which was absolutely devastating, in a thick wool sweater and jeans that sat perfectly on his hips.

Enough! she scolded herself. She quickly averted her eyes. She had already given up Aaron Mendel—of course, that had been before she'd discovered Lara in Lucas's room. In fact, the previous night seemed to belong to another era altogether. . . .

". . . isn't she, Zoey?" Aaron was asking.

"Huh?" Zoey's head jerked up. She knew her face was getting red again. "Sorry—I'm . . . uh, a little out of it."

He grinned wryly. "I said, Lara is supposed to be here right now, isn't she, Zoey?"

Before Zoey could even open her mouth, Claire said, "Lara got plastered this morning. Zoey sent her home. I'm subbing." The words popped out of her mouth like gunfire.

Aaron's eyes widened. "Lara got *what* this morning?"

"Drunk," Claire stated coldly. "I'm sure you're familiar with the term."

All of a sudden he laughed. "What's *that* supposed to mean, Claire?"

Claire's gaze hardened. "Nothing, Aaron. Why should it mean anything?"

"I don't know." Aaron shrugged. "You sound so accusatory. It's not like *I* got trashed this morning."

A harsh smile formed on Claire's lips. "But you *do* drink."

Zoey blinked a few times. The sudden, rapid exchange between these two was making her extremely tense. "Aaron doesn't drink, Claire," she said, mostly to interrupt them.

"Please." Claire chuckled snidely. "Did *he* tell you that?"

Zoey thought for a minute. The truth was, she couldn't remember whether he had ever mentioned drinking or not. But it didn't seem in keeping with his character. *She* had never seen him drink. Besides, he didn't even believe in premarital sex.

"What's your problem, Claire?" Aaron suddenly snapped. "Did you get a bad night's sleep or something?"

"Watch it, Aaron," Claire warned. "I'm serious."

"So am I," he replied. "We've got nothing to hide here."

"Would you please tell me what is going on?" Zoey cried, stepping out from behind the cash register. "Why are you two in a fight?"

Aaron's expression abruptly mellowed. "I'm sorry, Zoey," he said. His eyes flickered over to Claire. "I guess things are just a little weird between us."

"Why?"

"Our parents are on the verge of getting married, Zoey," Claire said dully. She wouldn't stop staring at Aaron. "It makes for a little tension, you know?"

Zoey looked from one to the other, then back again. She was all too familiar with tension between new siblings—but this seemed different. *Very* different.

"Which reminds me of the reason I'm here," Aaron said. "Your father and my mother have decided to throw a New Year's Eve party at your house." He sounded horrified at the prospect, but he smiled sweetly at Zoey. The combination was disarming. "I wanted to personally invite Zoey myself," he added.

Zoey swallowed.

"How thoughtful," Claire hissed.

"Well, I'll see you there, then. Oh, yeah—it's pot-luck, so bring whatever you want." Aaron turned and slammed the door behind him.

Zoey looked at Claire, who was still gazing vacantly at the door.

"What was that all about?" Zoey asked. "I mean, what was that *really* all about, Claire?"

"Nothing." Claire shook her head. "But let me give you some advice, Zoey, okay? Friend to friend. Aaron Mendel is not what he appears to be. Not by a long shot."

Jake plodded up the garage stairs to Lara's room, dreading what he was about to find. He could hear a monotonous hip-hop drumbeat pounding from behind her closed door. She was there, all right. He took a deep breath, placed his hand on the knob, and threw the door open.

Lara was dancing alone in the middle of her room, swaying slowly to the rhythm of the music. Her eyes were closed and her arms were waving high above her head. With the exception of a cut-off T-shirt and a pair of flimsy red underpants, she was wearing absolutely nothing. A bottle of vodka sat by the foot of her bed. It was nearly empty.

"Lara!" he barked.

Her eyes popped open. "Jakie!" she cried happily. She rushed over to him and threw her arms around his neck, breathing her stale, vodka-saturated breath into his face. He bristled, pulling away.

"What's up?" she slurred, looking at him slightly cross-eyed. "Aren't you happy to see me?"

Jake grabbed her arms firmly and removed them from his shoulders. "I thought you were supposed to work at the restaurant today," he said.

"Oops." Lara's arms flopped to her sides, and she staggered over to the stereo. When she couldn't find the volume knob, she gave up and collapsed onto her bed. "You're in one of those serious moods, aren't you?"

Jake stormed across the floor and jabbed a finger into the stereo's power button, instantly blanketing the room in silence. "You're damn right I am."

"Come on, Jakie," she sang. Her eyelids fluttered, then closed. "Don't be ser . . . don't be serious. It's Friday."

"Lara, it's not even five o'clock!" he shouted. "It's still light out!"

71

She giggled. "Well, you know the old saying. It's five o'clock somewhere. . . ."

Jake picked the bottle off the floor with a trembling hand. His knuckles whitened as he gripped it. He had to get her out of there before Zoey got home. He had to get her to somewhere safe.

"Why don't you have a drink?" Lara asked. "Let's have some fun."

"Lara, put on your clothes," he ordered, putting the bottle down. "You're coming home with me right now."

Her eyes popped open. "Hey, that's more like it!" she shouted, a little too loudly. "I like a man who takes charge!"

Jake's eyes flashed across the room. Clothes and CDs and garbage were strewn everywhere. He picked up a crumpled pair of jeans and shoved them into her face. "Put these on," he commanded.

"Nuh-uh," she said. Suddenly she grabbed his hand and yanked it—hard. Jake toppled on top of her onto the bed. She shrieked with laughter. "*Now* we're having fun!"

Jake furiously clawed his way off the mattress and rolled onto the floor with a painful thump.

"Where'd you go?" she cried, still laughing. "Come back here!"

But Jake was already stumbling to his feet and running for the door. This was too much. He'd never seen her so drunk. And he *wouldn't* let her talk him into splitting the rest of the bottle with her, as she'd done in the past. He'd learned his lesson. No, desperate situations called for desperate measures. He couldn't deal with her on his own. If he tried to subdue her himself, he might end up hurting her—or vice versa. He needed help.

"Hey, where are you going?" she yelled as he clattered down the stairs and bolted out the door.

Lucas couldn't stand being in his house alone for a second longer. He'd been moping around listlessly all day, feeling sorry for himself. The sun had nearly set. It was Friday night. The time had come to take some drastic action . . . maybe even get into a little trouble. It was time to get off the island for a while.

"Lucas?" his father called from the first floor.

Lucas groaned inwardly. The only time his father ever talked to him these days was when he wanted something. Come to think of it, the only time the old man talked to *anyone*—including his wife—was when he wanted something.

"Can't talk now," Lucas yelled as he headed downstairs. He grabbed his coat and black wool cap out of the front hall closet. "I'm meeting some people in Weymouth. I can't miss the five-ten ferry."

"You didn't tell me you were—"

Lucas slammed the door behind him.

The icy wind felt good against his face as he ran down Climbing Way, turning left onto Center Street. He glanced over the top of the Passmores' house at the ferry landing. The ferry was just pulling in from Allsworthy; he could see the lights of Weymouth twinkling beyond. *Perfect timing*, he thought. He hadn't even lied to his father, he realized with a smile. He *was* going to catch the 5:10 ferry to meet some people. He just wasn't sure which people. Not yet, anyway.

Maybe I'll give K-Berger a call, he thought. A smile played on his lips. Yes—she would be the perfect girl to help him take his mind off Zoey. She'd certainly expressed her interest in him on many previous occasions. And she was always looking for a good time.

When he turned left onto South Street, he paused for a moment. Jake was sprinting toward him. Even in the uncertain light of the streetlamps, Lucas could tell that something was seriously wrong. Jake's face looked terror-stricken.

"Lucas?" Jake yelled breathlessly. He skidded to a halt in front of him. "Man, am I glad I caught you. I was just coming to get you."

"You were?" Lucas asked. Suddenly he felt nervous. "Why? What's up?"

"Lara's on a binge right now. She's out of control. I need to get her to my place."

Lucas frowned. Why did Jake need his help for *that*? Lucas had already learned his lesson: Helping Lara McAvoy was *not* a wise move.

"You gotta help me, man," Jake said. "This is serious."

"You need my help?" Lucas shook his head and walked past him. "You're the football player, Jake. I'm sure you're strong enough to deal with Lara—"

Jake's hand clamped down on his shoulder.

"Hey!" Lucas jerked free and whirled to face him. "What the hell's your problem?"

"I need your help," Jake repeated, meeting his gaze. "Believe me, Cabral, I wouldn't ask for your help if I didn't need it."

Lucas opened his mouth—then hesitated. As much as he wanted to punch Jake McRoyan at that moment, he realized Jake was telling the truth. Jake *wouldn't* ask for his help if he didn't need it. A thought dawned on him: Lara was supposed to be working at Passmores'. She was at home, drunk, instead. Maybe this *was* serious,

"Are you gonna help me?" Jake demanded impatiently.

A fleeting vision of Louise Kronenberger flashed through his mind. He could just see her, smiling her sexy smile with a beer in one hand.

Why was it that he never seemed to get what he wanted?

"All right," he said resignedly, knowing with certainty that his night had already been ruined. "Let's go."

Aisha

I'm not worried about the future. I'm obsessed by it. I can't stop thinking about what's going to happen to my life. And the worst part of it is that there is no solution. Any decision I make has its own terrible consequences.

If I decide to say yes to Christopher, what would that mean? First of all, my parents would be completely horrified. They wouldn't come to the wedding. They would probably disown me. Do I want to elope to become a disowned teenage bride? If that happens, it essentially means that I become just another statistic; after all, I'm African American. I know that sounds cold and impersonal, but I can't help it. I swore to myself that I wouldn't be a statistic. It's a promise I can't break.

Besides, what will being married do to my chances of getting into college? What will that do to any kind of career I might want to pursue?

On the other hand, if I decide not to marry him, I'll be losing the one sure thing in my life right now. There is no other man for me but him; I know that. If my answer is no, Christopher Shupe will most likely walk out of my life forever on January fifth. And is a life without Christopher even worth living?

So, in a nutshell, the future is bleak. And time is running out. New Year's Eve is fast approaching.

I kind of look at it as choosing between the firing squad and the electric chair. Either way I'm screwed.

Nine

At ten-thirty Aisha yanked the last tissue out of the box on her dresser. She wiped her red, stinging eyes and sore nose, then tossed the tissue into the wastebasket, which had long since overflowed. She'd gone through the entire box in about three hours.

She simply couldn't stop crying. It was ridiculous; it wasn't as if anyone had *died* or anything. She needed to snap out of it. She needed to take her mind off Christopher, if only for a little while. A phone call would probably do the trick. Zoey would be getting home from work any minute, and Aisha could listen to all of Zoey's problems and forget about her own. It was amazing how someone else's misery could make one feel better about oneself.

She grabbed the phone off the nightstand and punched in the number, then leaned back in bed.

"Hello?" Zoey answered.

"Hey." She sniffed. "It's Eesh."

"Hey, what's wrong? Are you okay?"

Aisha laughed. "Aside from being hopelessly confused, sure."

There was a moment of silence on the other end. "I wish I could help you out," Zoey said finally. "But to be honest, I envy you."

"*Envy* me? Wow—you must have had a really bad day."

"How'd you guess?" she grumbled.

"What happened?"

"Well, let's see. I found Lucas and Lara together last night; Lara came to work drunk and I had to throw her out; Benjamin won't get his bandages off for a week—"

"Whoa, whoa," Aisha cut in. "Start from the beginning. You found *what* last night?"

"I went over to Lucas's late last night, and *she* was in his room, practically sitting on his lap."

Aisha hesitated. "Sitting or *practically* sitting?"

Zoey sighed. "Well, they were sitting next to each other, anyway. Both of them deny anything more than that."

"Hmmm . . ."

"What?"

"Is it possible they're telling the truth?" Aisha suggested as delicately as she could.

"Well, Christopher said that Lucas told him about it. Apparently Lucas denied everything to *him*, too. I know Christopher wouldn't lie, but Lucas . . ."

"But why would Lucas lie to Christopher?"

"Come on, Eesh." Zoey sounded exhausted.

"To prevent the inevitable—Christopher's telling you, then your telling me."

"I don't know," Aisha said doubtfully.

Suddenly Zoey laughed. "You know, you're right. Lucas doesn't think that far ahead. He's too focused on the here and now. He's too caught up with how he's possibly going to get me to sleep with him."

"Oh, it's not that bad."

"It *is* that bad, Eesh. I mean, why can't he be just

a little more like Aaron? Aaron doesn't even believe in premarital sex.''

Aisha bit her lip. She'd been debating all day whether or not to tell Zoey about finding Claire in the hall that morning. Given Zoey's current frame of mind, it probably wouldn't be the best idea. Then again, if she found out about it some other way . . .

"Eesh? You still there?"

"Yeah." She took a deep breath. "Look, Zoey, I'm going to tell you something. But you have to promise me you'll take it at face value and not read too much into it."

"Uh-oh," Zoey breathed. "I don't like the sound of this."

"This morning I saw Claire in the front hall. She was coming down the steps from Aaron's room."

"And?" Zoey asked, clearly unimpressed. "So what?"

"My room is right next to the steps, Zoey. I never heard her come in." Aisha sat up in bed, twirling the phone cord around her fingers. "And she was a complete mess. She looked like she had slept in her clothes. She was also totally freaked that I saw her."

"Oh, my . . ." Zoey's voice trailed off.

Aisha collapsed back onto her pillow. "That was my reaction."

Zoey laughed bitterly. "You know, it makes sense," she said after a moment. "Aaron came into the restaurant today, and there was all this weird tension between him and Claire."

Aisha didn't say anything. She didn't know what *to* say.

"You think they did it?" Zoey demanded.

"I don't know, Zoey, it's not—"

"I should have listened to Nina and Benjamin,"

Zoey muttered, obviously not listening. "They told me he was bad news. Claire said the same thing, as a matter of fact. And *she* had the nerve to tell me she was giving me advice 'friend to friend.' That's a laugh."

"Did, uh, she and Aaron come in together?" Aisha asked.

"No. Claire was subbing for Lara." Zoey's voice hardened. "You know, for a while today I actually thought I'd been all wrong about Claire. But I wasn't. Nina's right—she *is* the ice queen."

Aisha swallowed. She was beginning to regret that she had opened her big mouth. Zoey was working herself into a frenzy.

"Come on, Zoey. Claire isn't *that* bad. She subbed for Lara, right? Besides," she added hesitantly, "Aaron isn't your boyfriend. He wasn't cheating on you."

"Like that makes a difference?" Zoey cried.

"It does, believe it or not. I mean, when you were making out with Aaron, who was cheating on whom?"

"But—but—" Zoey spluttered.

"Sorry," Aisha said quietly. "I don't mean to be harsh."

"No. I'm just pissed because you're right." Zoey's tone grew calmer. "*And* that Claire and Aaron lied to me."

"They didn't lie to you; they just didn't tell you the whole truth," Aisha pointed out. "Besides, when it comes right down to it, can you blame Aaron? You've been giving him mixed signals, and Claire is . . . well, *there.* You should know by now that guys can't control their hormones."

"Christopher can," Zoey countered.

That was true, Aisha realized. But that hadn't always been the case. After all, she had walked in on him with another girl once, too.

"Eesh, you don't know how lucky you are to have a guy like him," Zoey went on. "He's so awesome."

"Yeah, but even he makes mistakes," Aisha said. That painful lump in her throat was returning. "*Nobody's* perfect," she continued hurriedly. "I mean, if you ask me, I think that you and Lucas still belong together."

Zoey was silent.

"But enough about boys," Aisha moaned. "Look, I'd better go. Wait a minute—by the way, what did happen with Lara today?"

"She started having cocktails at eleven this morning—and didn't stop until Jake found her at around five."

"Jeez," Aisha breathed. "Is she okay?"

"Well, she's sleeping at Jake's house right now. Jake and Lucas dragged her there."

"Jake and Lucas?" Aisha raised her eyebrows. "That's an unlikely duo."

"Yeah," Zoey mumbled. "Mr. McRoyan just called to tell me about it. He sounded as surprised as you. He said Jake wouldn't have been able to help Lara if it hadn't been for Lucas."

"See?" Aisha said meaningfully.

"See what?"

"Christopher may be awesome, but Lucas is an awesome guy, too."

Lucas took one last long look at Lara sprawled out on Jake's bed, then followed Jake out the door and closed it behind him.

"That sucked," Jake whispered.

Lucas was still too shocked to do anything more than just nod. For the past five hours they'd been huddled with Lara in the bathroom, cleaning her up every time she vomited. And when she had finally gotten rid of everything in her stomach, she'd begun to lash out incoherently. Nobody was spared. Lucas was a prude. Jake was a bastard. Zoey was a slut. Benjamin was a freak. Lucas was just thankful that she'd eventually gotten Chatham Island out of her system and started in on people he'd never heard of before.

"I'm really, really sorry, man," Jake muttered as they headed up the stairs. "I had no idea it would be like that."

Lucas shrugged. "I've seen worse things."

Mr. McRoyan was waiting for them in the living room, hunched forward on a long couch. His face was creased with exhaustion and worry.

"She asleep?" he asked gruffly.

Jake nodded.

Mr. McRoyan gestured toward an easy chair. "Have a seat, Lucas."

Lucas hesitated. "Uh, no, thanks, Mr. McRoyan," he said awkwardly. "It's pretty late, and I'm really, really tired. I think I should probably go home. My dad will be getting worried."

Jake slumped down next to his father. For a moment Lucas was taken by how much they looked alike, with their stocky frames and short, wiry brown hair. It was fitting, somehow. The resemblance was more than skin deep. Both were cold, and both knew how to hold a grudge.

"Well, let me at least give you a ride," Mr. McRoyan offered. "It's cold out there tonight."

"No, really, that's all right," Lucas said, unconsciously inching toward the front door. Just being in that house made him feel creepy. He hadn't been there in over two years—not since before Wade's death. He didn't belong; he felt too strange. "I could use the fresh air," he added.

"Wait." Mr. McRoyan stood and marched over to Lucas, gripping his hand firmly. "I just wanted to tell you how much I appreciate what you did tonight. You didn't have to come here. And you certainly didn't have to stay."

Lucas stared at his feet. "It was no big deal."

"Yes, it was. It was for a lot of reasons." Mr. McRoyan released his hand. "Look at me, Lucas."

Lucas felt sick. He didn't want to deal with confronting the past. Hadn't he already suffered enough that night? He woefully raised his head.

"I never had a chance to apologize to you for what happened between our families," Mr. McRoyan began. His voice was low and somber. "I don't agree with what you did—lying about your part in it—but I can understand your reasons." He cleared his throat. "That being said, I know that before the accident, you were very close to both of my boys. And in spite of everything, I sincerely hope you remain friends with Jake. You're always welcome here, Lucas. You're a good influence."

Lucas licked his lips, at a complete loss for words. A good influence? He'd never been called anything remotely similar in his entire life. A bastard, yes, a lazy bum, sure—but that was about it. How absurd it was that Mr. McRoyan, of all people, would be the first to label him "a good influence."

He glanced over at Jake. Jake was looking down, but Lucas could just see the faint beginnings of a tired grin. The irony of that comment wasn't lost on him, either.

Mr. McRoyan smiled. "You sure you don't want a ride home, son?"

Son? This was almost too much. Lucas took another step back. Jake finally looked up at him. His lips were twitching, almost as if he was trying to keep from laughing.

"No, thanks, Mr. McRoyan," Lucas said. "I'll be fine." He grabbed his black cap out of his coat pocket and pulled it over his head. "I'll see you later."

"Hey, Lucas," Jake called suddenly.

Lucas paused. "Yeah?"

"I'll give you a call tomorrow—you know, about Lara," he added quickly.

Lucas nodded. "Do that."

For a moment, just before he left, Lucas actually felt glad Mr. McRoyan had said his piece. He'd never imagined it would come out like that. He shook his head. His night hadn't been completely ruined after all.

Zoey lay rigidly in the darkness, staring straight up at her ceiling. Once again she couldn't sleep. Her mind was squirming with visions of her friends' faces, images of the recent past that had been frozen like snapshots: Claire's face when she had seen Aaron come into the restaurant that day, Jake's face when he had been holding Lara's bottle of tequila, Lucas's face when he had been caught with Lara.

The images faded, leaving only Lucas's face—his sleepy brown eyes and long, unruly blond hair.

"Lucas is an awesome guy, too."

She knew that now. Or had she known it all along? She felt as if there had always been something about him that she couldn't quite trust . . . but maybe she'd just been projecting an aspect of herself onto him. She didn't trust herself a lot of the time. But when she was with Lucas, she did.

Yes, Aaron had briefly driven her crazy—but she

knew now that it had been mostly the result of an intense physical attraction. She'd projected what she'd wanted onto him, too. She had romanticized him to the point of perfection. And when it came right down to it, Nina had been right: He was just a fairly sleazy guy with a talent for playing the guitar.

But there was nothing sleazy about Lucas. There was nothing shameful or dishonest about him. Sure, he wanted to sleep with her, but he told her exactly what was on his mind. She grinned sadly. He told her all the time, in fact. No, the only thing Lucas had in common with Aaron was that he was very, very sexy—but in a far more elusive way.

She felt an overwhelming urge to call him. It wasn't that late—just past eleven. If she called him, she could prevent the situation between them from getting any more out of hand. She could simply apologize, and that would be that.

Just as the thought occurred to her, there was a soft crunching noise outside her window—footsteps on the gravel in front of her house.

In an instant she was out of bed and running down the stairs. When she hit the last step, the doorbell rang.

"Who is it?" she asked hopefully.

"Aaron," came the reply.

"Aaron?" A black cloud of disappointment settled over her. "It's a little late, don't you think?"

"I know you're up, Zoey," he said teasingly. "I heard you coming down the stairs."

Suddenly she was filled with anger and loathing. "So what?" she demanded. "I didn't invite you here."

"Come on, let me in," he begged. "It's cold."

"I know it's cold. You should have thought of that before you came over. Haven't you ever heard of a telephone?"

There was a pause. "What's the matter?" he asked suspiciously. "Did Claire say something to you?"

"No, Aaron." She shook her head in disgust. "Claire didn't say anything."

"Let me in, Zoey," he repeated. "Please."

"I will if you quit whining," she breathed. It wouldn't hurt to let him in for thirty seconds. In fact, it would be just long enough to tell him to get lost— for good. She unlatched the bolt.

Aaron hurried inside and closed the door behind him, grinning broadly. "Well, it's about time," he said, sniffling. His nose was red from the cold. For some reason it made the rest of his face seem very pale.

Zoey folded her arms across her chest, feeling painfully self-conscious. She was wearing only loose sweatpants and a T-shirt. "What do you *want,* Aaron?" she asked crossly.

He shrugged. "To talk to you."

"In the middle of the night?"

"Come on, Zoey, it's only eleven." He smirked. "Besides, I know you're alone." He began to take his coat off.

"Don't make yourself too comfortable, Aaron," she warned.

Aaron paused, one arm already out of the coat. "What?" he asked, looking puzzled.

"Aaron, what does my being alone have to do with anything?"

He smiled and finished removing his coat. "I just thought you could use some company."

"You thought wrong." Looking at him now, Zoey wondered how she ever could have fallen for him. He was gorgeous, but so damn full of himself. Why couldn't she have seen it before? "Stop undressing," she ordered.

He leaned forward. "You really want me to do that?" he whispered.

"If you don't, I'm gonna call Lucas and Jake and Christopher," she whispered back. "Then they're gonna come over here and beat the crap out of you. How does that sound?"

His expression soured. "What did you say?"

"You heard me."

He laughed nervously. "You wouldn't do that."

"Oh, yeah? Try me."

"What the hell's gotten into you, Zoey?" he asked, pulling his coat back on.

"What's gotten into me is that I'm asking you to leave," Zoey snapped. "And I don't want you to come over here again unless you have an invitation."

He shook his head. "Come on," he prodded in a low, husky voice. "There's something between us, Zoey. You know—"

"There's *nothing* between us, Aaron."

"Well, what about the tape?" he demanded, suddenly angry. "What about the harmonica?"

"Is *that* it?" Zoey cried, appalled. "You thought you could *buy* me with your presents?"

"No, no . . . that's not what I meant. *You* gave me a present, too, you know—that blues book."

"You're absolutely right. And I hope you have fun with it, playing all those sad songs. Why don't you go home and learn a couple right now?" She reached for the door.

"What about the songs I wrote for you?" he protested.

Zoey froze. Why did he have to bring *that* up? "They were nice," she admitted quietly. "Look, Aaron, it's late. I have a big day tomorrow, all right?"

88

"But I wrote those songs for you, because I . . . because . . ."

"Because *what*, Aaron?" she asked, enraged again. "Because you wanted to sleep with me?"

He shook his head rapidly. "No, I told you—"

"You don't believe in sex before marriage," Zoey finished for him. "Give me a break. If you could see the phony look on your face right now, you wouldn't believe you, either."

"Okay, I give up!" he shouted, throwing his hands in the air. "What's so bad about sex, anyway?"

Zoey could only laugh. He was a liar and a fake, and he knew she knew it. She pulled the door open. "Nothing, Aaron. Nothing at all. In fact, I have a great idea. Claire isn't a virgin. Go write a song for her— you'll have better luck."

Using both hands, Zoey shoved him out the door, then slammed it in his wide-eyed, open-mouthed face.

Ten

The Countdown to
New Year's Eve

TEN . . .

Saturday morning at the Passmores'

Mr. Passmore arrives just as Mr. McRoyan and Jake show up with Lara. Mr. McRoyan suggests that Lara join Jake at his Alcoholics Anonymous meetings. Mr. Passmore agrees. Zoey suggests that Lara find another place to live. Despite sobbing protests from Lara and promises never to drink again, Mr. Passmore surprisingly agrees to that as well. "You have to prove that you respect our family before you can be a part of it," he says.

NINE . . .

Saturday afternoon at the Grays'

Aisha's parents confront her on why she's been so upset recently. She admits that Christopher is leaving Chatham Island in a few days to join the army but offers no further explanation. Later she confides to Kalif, her fourteen-year-old brother, that Christopher has asked her to marry him. After agreeing to death by strangulation if he tells anyone, Kalif enthusiastically approves of the marriage, citing the fact that "Christopher is dope."

EIGHT . . .

Saturday night at the Cabrals'

Lucas gets a call from Christopher: Does he want to go see a movie in Wcymouth? Sure, Lucas says, but why isn't Christopher hanging out with Eesh? Because she'll just drive him crazy, Christopher replies. Lucas can see where he's coming from. Girls will definitely drive a man crazy.

Lucas gets a call from Jake: Lara is getting kicked out of the Passmores' house. The two of them wonder if she remembers calling Lucas a prude. Lucas mentions that he and Christopher are going to Weymouth, but Jake declines to join them. Lucas reminds Jake that he's a good influence. Jake changes his mind and decides to come along. He states the obvious: It's pathetic that three guys are going to the movies alone on a Saturday night. Lucas reminds Jake that if they had girls to hang out with, they would.

Lucas gets a call from Zoey just as he's walking out the door. He tells his father to tell her that he's already gone.

SEVEN . . .

Sunday morning at the Geigers'

After enduring an endless party-planning brunch

with her father, Aaron, and Tattoo (her new term for Aaron's mother, after the dwarf on *Fantasy Island*), Claire retires to her room for some much-needed solitude. Aaron barges in after her and starts blaming her for ruining things with Zoey. Claire very calmly tells him to shut up. She adds that he's welcome to stay up there so long as they discuss ozone depletion in the ionosphere. He leaves.

SIX . . .

Sunday afternoon at the McRoyans'

Mr. McRoyan invites Louise Kronenberger back to the house for dinner after Jake's second AA meeting. Much to Jake's dismay, Louise and Mr. McRoyan seem to hit it off very well. After dinner, Louise lingers in Jake's room and asks if he's seeing anyone. Jake says he is—but that his girlfriend still has some real problems. He tells her what happened with Lara on Friday night. Louise warns him that it's not wise for a former alcoholic to see someone who still drinks.

FIVE . . .

Sunday night at the Chatham Island Apartments

Christopher is unexpectedly awakened by Lara, who apologizes profusely for her behavior on Friday. Without referring to Christopher as "man" once, Lara asks when he is moving out of his cozy little room on the third floor, and Christopher tells her he'll be leaving in a week. Lara asks if she can take over his lease. Christopher promises he'll talk to his landlord in the morning.

FOUR . . .

Monday morning at Boston General Hospital
After an exhaustive two-hour examination, Dr. Martin informs Benjamin that his bandages will have to stay on a little longer than expected and that he will get them off January fifth. Apparently there was some minor complication—nothing terribly serious, he says, and Benjamin should try not to worry. Later, Benjamin and Nina fight over whether Nina should go back to Chatham Island before he gets his bandages off. Benjamin claims she's pitying him again. Nina finally compromises on January fourth.

THREE . . .

Monday afternoon at Passmores'
Claire appears at the restaurant and asks Mr. Passmore if he needs any help. He thanks her but says that Lara is working and that so far she seems to be okay. Claire pulls Zoey aside and apologizes for not telling her about sneaking over to visit Aaron. Zoey curtly informs Claire that if she wants him, she can have him. Later Lucas shows up to talk to Christopher. Zoey offers him a piece of cake. He curtly informs her he isn't hungry.

TWO . . .

Monday night in the guest wing of Gray House

Aaron is alone in his room, playing songs from Zoey's book, when Claire unexpectedly knocks. "Here to lead me on again?" he asks. Claire sarcastically replies that she's there to retrieve the book she lent him—*The Greenhouse Effect: Global Warming and Its Consequences*—and would he like to discuss it? No, but he just found a song about Claire that he'd like to perform: "Evil Woman Blues." The two of them trade insults for the next three hours.

ONE!

Tuesday morning on board the Minnow
*(the island kids' nickname for the ferry, after
the unlucky boat in* Gilligan's Island)

Much to their collective horror, Jake, Christopher, and Lucas run into Zoey and Aisha belowdecks. A terse and largely monosyllabic exchange reveals that both groups are on their way to the mall to buy items for the big party that night.

Lucas: cheese
Christopher: cake
Jake: sparkling cider
Zoey: snacks (unspecified)
Aisha: more cheese

The boys quickly return to the upper deck, where they endure a wind chill of minus fifteen degrees for the remainder of the twenty-minute ride to Weymouth. After carefully avoiding the girls at the mall, the boys accidentally meet them again on the ferry during the return trip to Chatham Island.

Eleven

By the time Zoey reached her front walk with her shopping bag full of caviar, smoked salmon, and gourmet bread sticks, she felt as if her arms were about to fall off. But the physical pain she felt was far preferable to the emotional pain she had endured during her little expedition to the mainland. Never before had she felt so *ignored*.

Why was Lucas being so cruel? She could understand if Christopher wanted to avoid Aisha, and even that he would want support from his male buddies. Guys loved to act like wolves in a pack; it gave them a weird, false sense of strength. But she couldn't understand why Lucas had been looking at her the way he had . . . as if she were not fit to be on the same boat as he was—or even the same planet.

Well, there was no point in dwelling on it. Everything would get cleared up that night at the party.

"I'm home," she called, staggering through the front hall toward the kitchen. She caught a glimpse of Lara and her father sitting at the table in the breakfast nook, then let her bag slam down on the kitchen counter.

"Was the trip a success?" Mr. Passmore asked.

"I wouldn't call it that," Zoey mumbled. "I did get everything I wanted, though."

"Zoey, can you come in here for a minute, please?"

Zoey winced. The last thing she felt like doing was talking to her father and Lara. All she wanted was to go upstairs and flop down on her bed.

"Good news, Zoey," Lara announced. "I'm moving out January fifth." Her voice was void of emotion.

"Oh." Zoey sat down at the table. She had no idea what to say. "Congratulations" didn't seem appropriate, given the circumstances. She stared straight out the window at Lucas's house.

"She's going to move into Christopher's old place," Mr. Passmore said. "Isn't that convenient?"

"Um . . . yeah." For some reason Zoey was unable to bring herself to look Lara in the eye. When she'd first suggested that Lara move out, she'd been fraught with anger and exhaustion, and she hadn't expected that her father would so readily agree to the idea. Admittedly, she'd been pleasantly surprised. But now, with the move suddenly definite, she felt a strange guilt gnawing at her. After all, Lara *had* done a decent job at the restaurant the previous day. Had Zoey overreacted?

"Christopher was a big help," Lara added. "He gave me a good recommendation."

He did? Zoey was shocked—which made her feel even more guilty.

"Lara will continue to work at the restaurant," Mr. Passmore went on, almost as if Lara weren't there. "And when she starts going to AA meetings and really proves to us that she's sincere about straightening up, then we'll discuss her living situation again."

Zoey just kept looking straight ahead. She'd never heard her father talk that way—so formally and impersonally. If anyone's personality was antithetical to being formal, it was her father's. Even in tough situations in the past—even when he'd nearly broken up with Zoey's mother—he'd been able to joke, or at least smile. Then again, nothing about this situation was even remotely funny.

"I'm actually looking forward to living on my own," Lara said in the same unreadable tone. "I think it will be good for me." And with that she stood and left the table. A moment later the front door closed behind her.

Zoey shook her head. "Dad—"

"I know what you're going to say, Zoey," he interrupted. "You're going to say that you really don't want Lara to move out."

She had to laugh. "I'm *that* predictable, huh?"

"You say that as if it's a bad thing." Mr. Passmore placed his hand over hers. "The only reason you're so predictable is because you have the biggest heart of anyone I know."

"Dad, please." Zoey pulled her hand away. "Don't start with the clichés."

He sighed. "Let me tell you a little secret, Zoey. Even if you hadn't suggested that Lara move out, I would have. Having her here is too much of a strain on this household."

"But aren't you worried about her? When she's out on her own, she won't have *anyone*."

"That's not true. She'll still have us. She always will. I've made that abundantly clear from the moment she walked into our lives. But I won't allow her to take advantage of our family or our house. I expect the same from her as I do from you and Benjamin."

"I don't know. . . ." Zoey chewed a fingernail distractedly. "She's had such a rough time of it. . . ."

"I know she has." Mr. Passmore leaned forward. His deep blue eyes were thoughtful and intense. "But that's no excuse to abuse what we offer her. Our love is there. When she learns how to accept that love and reciprocate, we'll all be better off. Right now she has a little more growing and learning to do."

Zoey looked at him, fearful of what she was about to say. "You don't think that she'll just drink herself to death?" Her voice was barely a whisper.

He shook his head adamantly. "No, I truly don't. I think part of the reason she's been drinking so much recently is that she's confused. Think about it—for the first time in her life, she's been thrust into a situation where she has no responsibilities. Until now she's always had to fend for herself. Maybe she's feeling a little inadequate."

"So you're saying that booting her out of the house will make her feel better about herself?"

Mr. Passmore finally cracked a smile. "Well, when you put it *that* way . . ."

"Seriously, Dad," Zoey insisted.

"Seriously, I think that some time on her own will do her a world of good. She can reflect—and she'll *have* to shape up."

Zoey couldn't think of anything to say.

"Look," he added, "in a way, this is the best time for her to sort things out on her own. We have enough to worry about right now. If Benjamin . . ." He didn't finish.

"I know," Zoey whispered. "I know."

"Lara McAvoy is a survivor, Zoey. Trust me." He smiled again. "Everyone in our family is."

I wish that were true, she thought, looking out the window at Lucas's house, perched up on the hill. Just then *she* didn't feel like a survivor at all. She felt much more like a casualty.

"Thank you so much for all your help, Claire," Sarah Mendel chirped happily, surveying the decorations in the front hall. "I think this party is going to be very, very special."

"Oh, it's nothing," Claire said politely. "I'm happy to help you." *And I'd be happy to kill you, too*, she added to herself.

She had just spent the past three hours helping Mrs. Mendel tape up ribbons, blow up balloons, and make a huge sign that read Happy New Year Chatham Island—all while Aaron and her father whooped it up in the kitchen. It seemed as if *they* were becoming best buddies. But if she had to spend another millisecond with Tattoo . . .

"Do you think there's anything else that needs to be done?" Mrs. Mendel asked, tapping her fingernail against her chin and looking around.

"I think we're fine," Claire said, already halfway up the stairs. "I'm just going to go to my room for a while." She turned and bolted up to the third floor.

Instead of staying in her room, she grabbed a couple of sweaters and a long scarf from her closet. Then she bundled herself up and proceeded up the ladder to the widow's walk.

The sun was just sinking behind the mainland, illuminating the sky above Weymouth with brilliant hues of pink, orange, and red. In spite of the freezing wind, Claire smiled happily. It had been at least three days since she'd been up to her private little sanctuary, the one place on earth where she truly felt at peace. And that had been three days too long.

Tonight's the night, she said to herself, wrapping her

arms tightly around her body. *Tonight things are going to happen between Aaron and me.*

The previous night's visit had gone even better than expected. She suddenly laughed out loud. She and Aaron had both been on a roll. She'd never dished out or taken such verbal abuse—and she couldn't remember the last time she'd had so much fun.

No two people were more compatible. It was true. He was the perfect match for her. She thought of the other boys she'd loved—or thought she'd loved—but there was no comparison.

Lucas had been charming but naive. When he had been her boyfriend, before the accident, he'd been something of a rebel, a troublemaker. He'd floated from one experience to the next without a care in the world. Now he was a little more serious, a little more responsible—but just as clueless. He was still searching for perfection because he truly believed perfection to exist.

Benjamin, on the other hand, was much more savvy. Like Aaron, he matched her intelligence and wit—but his humor was far darker. And in the end, his own inability to fully trust her had done them in as a couple. She'd always felt as if he'd been secretly hoping to discover some horrible secret about her. And when the truth came out about Wade's accident, he'd suspected she'd known it all along.

And lastly there was Jake. Poor Jake. Handsome, honest . . . but when you came right down to it, not very bright. Jake wasn't adept at concealing his emotions; he was unable to grasp what it meant to communicate one thing by saying another. For him, everything had to be spelled out in three-foot-high letters.

But Aaron was far different.

He never said anything *directly*—that was what she liked most about him. There was always some hidden meaning, some subtext. He was a master at playing games with his words.

It also didn't hurt that he was probably the best-looking boy she had ever seen.

Yes, there was a chemistry between them. That had been confirmed the night before. Aaron had been used to dealing with potential girlfriends as inferiors—just as she had with *her* potential boyfriends. That girl Julia was a perfect example. But he had met his match in Claire, and he knew it. Neither of them could take advantage of the other.

The sun was nearly gone. It was almost time to get ready for the party.

Tonight's the night.

Aisha jerked awake with a start. Her room was very dark; she must have fallen asleep the moment she'd gotten home.

The remnants of a strange dream still clung to her. In it she'd been on a plane with Christopher. She'd been very distressed because a flight attendant kept trying to upgrade her ticket to first class. She refused, but Christopher encouraged her to go. "The seats are much bigger up there," he kept saying. "Go on, go on." The flight attendant's face kept changing, too. One second she looked like Zoey, the next like Nina, the next like her mother. Finally the flight attendant grabbed her and yanked her out of her seat.

That was when she'd woken up.

Aisha shivered. Dream analysis was *definitely* not her specialty, but she understood enough about psychology to know that the subconscious worked in powerful and often obvious ways. She knew she belonged with Christopher; that much was undeniable. So why was she hesitating? Did she think she was somehow too good for him?

"The seats are much bigger up there." Did *Christopher* think that she was too good for him?

No—that was impossible. She smiled in the darkness. Christopher Shupe didn't think *anyone* was too good for him. That was one of the many things she secretly loved about him.

She glanced at the glowing numbers on the clock by her bed. 6:19. The party was supposed to start at nine. She still hadn't made up her mind. The six days since she'd made her promise had abruptly shrunk to less than three hours, and she still had no idea what her answer would be.

Why couldn't she just receive some kind of divine signal? That would make things a lot easier. A huge, glowing pillar of fire that commanded her to marry Christopher would clear things up in a jiffy.

Maybe she would just wait for that to happen and skip the party altogether.

Christopher

AM I WORRIED ABOUT THE FUTURE? YEAH, I GUESS YOU COULD SAY THAT. I'M STILL WAITING FOR THE ANSWER THAT WILL DETERMINE WHETHER OR NOT MY LIFE IS RUINED. THAT'S JUST CAUSE FOR WORRY, ISN'T IT?

BEFORE I POPPED THE QUESTION, I WASN'T WORRIED IN THE LEAST. WELL, MAYBE JUST A LITTLE BIT-BUT NOT MUCH. SHE WAS GOING TO SAY YES, AND WE WERE GOING TO LIVE HAPPILY EVER AFTER. I WAS GOING TO BE A HUGELY SUCCESSFUL MAN, AND SHE WAS GOING TO BE MY HUGELY SUCCESSFUL WIFE.

SOUNDS PERFECT, DOESN'T IT?

IF SHE SAYS NO, I MAY STILL BE HUGELY SUCCESSFUL. BUT SUCCESS IS GOING TO SEEM PRETTY DAMN EMPTY AND MEANINGLESS WITHOUT HER.

IN A WAY, MY WHOLE LIFE UP UNTIL THIS POINT HAS BEEN ONE LONG SEARCH FOR PERFECTION. I'M LUCKIER THAN MOST: I FOUND IT, AND AT A PRETTY YOUNG AGE.

IF AISHA DENIES ME, I'LL LOSE THAT PERFECTION FOREVER. IT MAY TAKE ME ANOTHER EIGHTEEN YEARS TO FIND SOMETHING EVEN REMOTELY CLOSE AGAIN.

OR I MAY NEVER FIND IT.

Twelve

Christopher was the first to arrive at the party, impeccably dressed in the same dark suit he'd worn the night he'd proposed to Aisha. He gave Mrs. Mendel a kiss on the cheek and handed her the cake he'd bought earlier in Weymouth, then shook hands with Mr. Geiger.

Aaron and Claire were already in the living room, standing next to a table full of perfectly arranged food and looking bored out of their skulls. *What a pair*, Christopher thought dryly. They almost looked fake—like a couple of models out of a Calvin Klein ad who had been hired to look good at the party. Aaron was wearing a *tuxedo*, for crying out loud. And Claire was dressed to kill in a long, elegant strapless black dress that clung to every curve of her body.

So much for being the best-dressed guy here, he thought miserably. This was one night he was *not* in the mood for any competition.

Lucas was the next to arrive. He was wearing brown corduroy pants and an ill-fitting blazer he had borrowed from his dad. He shyly said hello to Mrs. Mendel and Mr. Geiger, then dumped his wheel of cheese on the living room table without bothering to take it out of the bag. He glanced around, but the only people there so far were Christopher, Claire, and Aaron.

"What's up, guys?" Lucas asked, trying hard not to notice how good Claire looked. He forced himself to shake hands with Aaron, then shook hands with Christopher, who rolled his eyes as if to say, "We're in for a long night."

"I—uh—I guess I miscalculated being fashionably late," Lucas said, feeling very underdressed.

"Don't worry, Lucas," Claire said skeptically, giving his outfit the once-over. "Nobody can say you aren't fashionable."

Leave it to Claire to make him feel right at home. He felt like hitting her over the head with his cheese.

Zoey came next, accompanied by Lara. She handed her bag of groceries to Mrs. Mendel, hugged and kissed Mr. Geiger, then introduced Lara to both of them. Zoey wore a formal blue dress that matched her eyes. Lara wore a black one that Mr. Passmore had lent her from Mrs. Passmore's closet. Zoey had felt as if Lara was somehow trespassing by wearing her mother's dress, but she kept her thoughts to herself.

Her heart sank the moment she walked into the living room. She'd been hoping Aisha would already be there, but she wasn't.

"Hey!" Zoey said, trying her best to sound happy.

Lucas grunted a hello without looking at her. Aaron shook her hand loosely, and Claire smiled her frigid smile. Christopher was the only one who showed any enthusiasm, hugging her and kissing her on the cheek.

Zoey continued to smile, feeling more awkward and lonely in that house than she ever would have imagined possible. Where were Nina and Benjamin when she needed them the most?

*　*　*

Jake arrived with his father and mother, both of whom were quickly swept off into the study with Mr. Geiger, Mrs. Mendel, and a few other forty-somethings. He was wearing the only suit he owned—a slightly constricting conservative black two-piece his father had bought him for college interviews. He stood alone in the hallway, lamely clutching his bottles of sparkling cider, until Zoey ushered him into the living room with a friendly wave.

"How's it going?" he whispered to her, glancing around. The party was just large enough to have formed two little conversational circles: one being Aaron and Claire, and the other being Lucas and Christopher. Lara stood silently by Zoey's side, staring at her feet. Her presence was actually a good sign, he realized. At least she wasn't home alone, wasted.

"How's it going?" Zoey repeated his question. "I don't want to get into that right now. Do you?"

Jake smiled. Good old Zoey. As long as she was there, the party might just be tolerable.

Aisha showed up around ten-thirty. She was wearing the same strapless black dress she'd worn the night Christopher had proposed. Her ears were instantly bombarded with raucous party sounds: roaring laughter, excited conversation, and glasses tinkling. The house was filled with people; her parents and Kalif were already there. Mrs. Mendel greeted her at the door and took her cheese, then informed her that "all of her buddies" were in the dining room.

All of my buddies, Aisha said to herself, suddenly short of breath.

That meant Christopher, too.

Thirteen

With less than an hour to go until midnight, Zoey found herself alone in the Geigers' huge kitchen. She wasn't exactly hiding—she just wasn't feeling very social. Of course, not too many people were feeling very social toward her, either.

"Hey, there you are," Aisha said, strolling through the door. "I've been looking for you." She paused, looking at Zoey confusedly. "What's wrong?"

"Nothing." She shrugged. "I guess I just don't feel like mixing and mingling."

Aisha nodded sympathetically. "I hear you."

"So what's going on? How come you're not with Christopher?"

Aisha shook her head. "Because I'm waiting until the last possible minute. I've been blowing him off all night."

"Eesh, that doesn't—"

"Let's not talk about it, all right?" She tried to smile. "How come *you're* not with Lucas?"

Zoey raised her eyebrows. "Lucas is pretending I don't exist, remember? I don't even know where he is."

"He's upstairs in Nina's room with Jake and Lara."

"What's up with Jake and Lucas, anyway?" Zoey asked, almost to herself. "When did they suddenly become best buddies?"

"Who knows?" Aisha raised her shoulders. "Maybe they're bonding over their little escapade with Lara the other night."

Zoey shook her head. They probably *were* bonding— but not over that. They were probably bonding over the fact that they had both gone out with Zoey and that both of their relationships had ended in failure. There was nothing like shared misery to bring people together, even people who had disliked each other as much as Lucas and Jake.

Claire walked into the kitchen, carrying an empty tray. "What's up, guys?" she asked breezily. "Having fun?" She put the tray down on the counter and opened the refrigerator.

"We're trying," Zoey said, trying very hard to sound gracious. "Do you need any help or anything?"

"Nah, I've pretty much got everything under control." She smiled as if she had just made a private joke with herself.

Zoey rolled her eyes at Aisha.

"Maybe we should go back into the party," Aisha said reluctantly. The phone started ringing. Claire closed the refrigerator and went to pick it up. "People might start to wonder."

"No one's been wondering about me—"

"Hey, you guys—it's Nina!" Claire hissed, momentarily cupping her hand over the mouthpiece of the phone. "So what's up?" Claire asked. "How's Benjamin?" She nodded gravely, then frowned. "Sure. Hold on a sec." She thrust the phone at Zoey.

Zoey ran over and snatched it out of Claire's hand with ill-disguised eagerness. "Hey, what's up?"

"Not much," Nina replied. Her voice sounded small and far away. "Benjamin, your mom, and I are watching *Rockin' New Year's Eve* on Fox. It's pretty wild, as you can imagine."

Zoey grinned. "Yeah," she whispered, glancing around furtively. Luckily Claire and Aisha had decided to clear the room and give her some privacy. "Well, you're not missing much, I can tell you that."

"What's the word on Eesh and Christopher?"

"None yet. She's been avoiding him all night."

"Uh-oh. Not a good sign."

"Yeah, well, who knows? How's Benjamin doing?"

"He's doing . . . all right." Nina sounded unsure. "A little impatient, but all right. He's right here. You want to talk to him?"

"In a sec." Zoey hesitated. "How are *you* doing?"

Nina laughed. "Me? Peachy."

"I heard from my dad that Benjamin is making you come back on the fourth."

"Jeez, Zo." Nina sighed. "I don't know if I really want to get into any lurid details about my problems with my boyfriend right—*ouch!*" She giggled. "Benjamin just slapped me!"

"So everything's okay?" Zoey asked.

"Maybe you should ask your brother. I'll talk to you later, Zo. Tell everyone happy New Year for me. Tell them I say they should all get slobberingly wasted and do a lot of things they won't remember in the morning."

Zoey laughed, wishing very much that Nina weren't three hundred miles away. "I'll do that. Have fun down there, okay?"

"I'll try. Bye."

There was a fumbling sound, then Benjamin's voice said, "Hello?"

"Hey," Zoey said, sounding as unconcerned as possible.

"How's it going up there? Any fights yet?"

"Very funny," Zoey replied. "I'm glad to see you still have your lame sense of humor."

"It's hard not to after spending four days straight with your mother and your girlfr—*yow!* Hey!" He laughed. "They're pounding on me with pillows," he explained.

"Sounds like fun," Zoey said wistfully.

"Nonstop fun, Zo. You should really get a dangerous experimental operation sometime. So Eesh still hasn't given her answer yet?"

"Not yet," Zoey said.

"I, uh, heard about Lara. Is she there?"

Zoey looked around instinctively, but Lara was nowhere in sight. "Yeah, she is. She's actually been pretty cool all night."

"Maybe she's on drugs. Hey, now that she's gone, I'll have something to look forward to when I come back."

"Benjamin!" Zoey exclaimed. "You were the one who was always telling *me* to give her a chance."

"That's the older brother's job, Zo," he said sarcastically. "You know, to give stupid advice. I don't have to actually mean what I say."

"I see. I'll remember that."

"Look, I'd better go. Mom sends . . . *what*?" He paused. "Hugs and kisses, and she'll call you tomorrow. Happy New Year."

"Happy New Year, Benjamin. I'm glad you called. Good luck."

"Thanks. I think I'm gonna need it. Bye." The line clicked.

Zoey hung up the phone. Once again she was by

herself. She had a sudden urge to sneak out of the house, hop on the ferry, and take a midnight bus to Boston.

But when it came right down to it, she probably wouldn't feel any better down there, either.

Claire walked slowly up the stairs, feeling a jittery anticipation. She'd seen Aaron in the foyer just before she'd gone into the kitchen. He hadn't even said anything. He'd just jerked his head toward the staircase and silently mouthed, "Your room?"

It could have been totally innocent, she realized as she rounded the corner on the second floor. Maybe he just wanted to discuss the logistics of the party. Maybe he just needed a breather.

Or maybe he had something else in mind.

Claire paused outside Nina's door. The muffled sounds of some grunge band were coming from Nina's stereo—and there was no conversation. Claire frowned. She didn't exactly like the idea of somebody using Nina's room as a makeout chamber, especially when Nina was in another state. Then again, better her little sister's room than her own.

"Hello?" she said, rapping lightly on the door. "Anyone home?"

"Come in," Lucas answered.

Claire pushed the door open. Lucas, Jake, and Lara were sprawled on the floor, excitedly rummaging through all of Nina's unlistenable CDs.

Now here's an interesting little threesome, Claire thought. *But now's not the time to involve myself in figuring out what's going on with them.*

"Glad to see you guys have made yourself at home," she said dryly. "I'm sure Nina would appreciate it."

"You know, I think I have a newfound respect for old Ninny," Jake said, clearly not listening to a word of what Claire was saying. He snatched a CD off the floor and held it up for her to see: Black Sabbath's *Paranoid*. Claire made a face.

"She's got discs I didn't even know *existed*," he added.

"Yeah, it's wild," Lucas concurred, studying the liner notes of another one.

Lara just smiled nervously.

"Well, I hope you all enjoy yourselves," Claire mumbled, feeling a vague revulsion. "Just be sure to put everything back." She pulled the door closed behind her and hurried up to the third floor.

When she reached the top of the stairs, she frowned.

Aaron was there, all right. But he wasn't exactly waiting with candles and champagne. He was sitting at her computer with his back to her.

"Hey, check this out!" he said, laughing and clicking her mouse. "Did you know that there was a Web site called 'Kill Jay Leno'?"

"No, I didn't," she answered wearily. She slouched down on her bed, feeling more than a little let down. What was going on with this party, anyway? Why was everyone behaving like five-year-olds?

Aaron shook his head. "It's the most ridiculous thing. . . ."

"Aaron, we're supposed to be hosting a party downstairs. The New Year starts in about forty-five minutes. Do you think this is the best time to be surfing the Internet?"

"Well . . . yeah, I do." He laughed again. "This is when all the real kooks come out and reveal themselves."

Claire smiled in spite of herself. She was glad that

113

he couldn't see her face. "I didn't know you were such a computer geek," she chided.

"Now you do." He shrugged nonchalantly. "You know I can't hide anything from you, Claire. Hey, listen to what these guys have to say: 'We don't even believe in Jay Leno. He doesn't exist. He is a hoax created by the United States Government to subjugate the—' "

But Claire couldn't listen. *"You know I can't hide anything from you, Claire."* What had he meant by that? Had it been that obvious she had been thinking the same thing about *him?*

"Aaron, why did you ask me to come up here?" she suddenly demanded.

"You know why I brought you up here."

The gravity of his tone made her heart lurch. She held her breath. He swiveled around in the chair and fixed her with an unblinking glare, his hazel eyes glistening in the soft light of the room.

"Why?" she repeated, swallowing.

"I had to prove to you, once and for all, that Jay Leno doesn't exist."

"Aaron!"

He grinned. "It's time to wake up to the facts, Claire. You've been living in a dream world."

She tried to maintain a straight face, but as much as she wanted to keep from laughing, she couldn't.

"Seriously, Claire, how else can I prove myself to you? Writing a song for you won't work, because you'll think it's phony. And I can't talk to you about the weather, because you know I don't give a crap about that. You just know me too well."

She looked up at him. Her laughter had died down. She couldn't tell what she was feeling anymore. She only knew she was hanging on his every word.

Aaron got up slowly and sat down next to her on the bed. He took her hand. "The only way I can prove to you that I'm not the most manipulative, cold-hearted liar in the world is by exposing the Jay Leno conspiracy." In spite of the absurdity of the remark, his voice was deadly serious. "It's the only choice I have left."

Claire stared into his eyes, now only inches away. They'd never looked so open and unguarded.

"I don't think you're a manipulative, cold-hearted liar," she whispered. "I never have."

"That's sweet. But it's a lie."

She smiled. "I guess you're right. But everything we tell each other is a lie."

He smiled back. "That's the way things are between us."

Her face drew closer to his, seemingly of its own volition. "It doesn't have to be that way," she pleaded.

"How can we change it?"

Claire squeezed his hand. "By being honest with each other."

"I'd like that. I really would."

"Will you kiss me?" she breathed.

Aaron closed his eyes. "I was hoping you'd ask me that. This conversation is getting much too complicated."

When all is said and done, Lucas read, *Aerosmith's legacy can be heard in the sound of every so-called alternative band today.*

He put the CD cover down. Suddenly he noticed that Lara and Jake were sitting much closer to each other than they had been two minutes before. Maybe now would be a good time to leave.

"See you guys later," he mumbled, quickly hopping

up from the floor. He closed the door behind him—and stopped.

Zoey had just rounded the corner. She froze in mid-step when she saw him.

They were face-to-face.

"Hey," he mumbled, looking over her shoulder down the narrow little hall at an empty guest room.

"Oh, hey." She looked at Nina's closed door. "I was—uh, just coming up to see what was going on in Nina's room."

He shrugged. "Jake and Lara are in there."

"Oh." She looked perturbed. "Do they want to be left alone?"

"I really don't know." He sidestepped her, raising his arms to avoid any contact. "Why don't you knock and see?"

"Lucas—wait."

He bent his head, casting a longing glance at the room in front of him. If only he had come out of Nina's room thirty seconds earlier, he could have walked straight into that room, closed the door, and hidden there for the rest of the night.

"Will you talk to me, Lucas?" Zoey begged. "Please?"

"Fine." He pointed limply toward the darkened doorway. "Let's go in there."

"I don't want to talk if it's going to be a chore for you," she said. Her voice cracked. "I don't want to ruin your good time."

Lucas turned to look at her. Her eyes were red, and she was blinking very rapidly. For a moment he stared at her face, but instead of experiencing the usual pangs of remorse, he found he was angry. Girls were so damn lucky. All a girl had to do was turn on the waterworks, then *bang*—instant forgiveness. Well, he was not going

116

to fall for that anymore. He'd been burned by Zoey's tears enough already.

"To be honest, Zoey, talking to you does have an uncanny habit of ruining my good time."

"How can you say that?" Her voice was quivering. "How can you just . . ." The rest of her words were lost in sobs.

Lucas just shook his head. *He* was the one who had tried so hard to make the relationship work, not her. With every effort he'd made, it seemed as if she'd just turned around and spat back in his face. If she couldn't see that, she had nobody to blame but herself.

"Look, Zoey," he said finally. "I know you're going through a rough time right now. I just don't think I'm the right person . . . to talk to you about it."

He opened his mouth to say something else—then turned and left her there, crying alone in the hall.

Fourteen

Jake was beginning to become acutely aware of the silence in the room. Well, not silence, exactly—Black Sabbath was still blaring—but the distinct lack of conversation. He concentrated hard on staring straight at Nina's stereo, trying to ignore Lara's breath on the back of his neck.

"Jake?" she whispered.

His body involuntarily tensed. "Yeah?"

"How come you haven't called me in the past few days?"

Jake abruptly stood and moved to Nina's bed. "I, uh . . . I've been kind of . . ."

Lara sat next to him. "Kind of blowing me off?"

He looked at her. "Lara, I'm really confused right now, all right? I've got a lot of things on my mind."

"And I don't?" Lara cried, pointing to herself. "I just got kicked out of my house, remember?"

"I remember," Jake shot back. The comment offended him; after all, *she* had gotten herself kicked out. Why was she always acting like a victim?

"What else do you remember, anyway?" he asked after a moment.

"Oh, boy . . ." She leaned back on her elbows, looking exasperated. "What's that supposed to mean?"

"Do you remember throwing up all over Lucas and me?" he shouted. "Do you remember calling me a bastard? Do you remember telling me you were going to burn all of Chatham Island to the ground? *Do you*?"

Lara's mouth fell open. Her jaw trembled, but she didn't say anything.

"Now you know why I haven't called you." He walked over to the stereo and turned the volume down, mostly so he wouldn't have to look at her face anymore.

"I told you I was sorry about that, Jake," she said tremulously. "I really am. . . ."

"Well, why don't you do something about it?" He whirled around to face her again. "Why don't you come to AA meetings with me? Why don't you do something nice for the Passmores—like send Benjamin a card? Or even just *apologize* to Lucas? Why don't you do something more than the bare minimum for once?"

A lone tear slid down Lara's cheek. "I'm trying, Jake." She blinked, then wiped her face with her hand. "It's hard for me."

"I know it is," he said, softening his tone. "But it's hard for me, too. And right now I think we need some time apart."

She nodded, sitting up straight. "You know, I haven't had a drink since Friday."

"Good. That's a start. But I'm telling you, Lara, you need help. You can't do it on your own. And if you come to these meetings with me, you won't even *want* to drink again. I know I don't."

She peered at him dubiously. "You're just saying that."

He shook his head. "Why won't you let yourself

trust someone? Anyone? For once in your life?''

"Why should I trust anyone?"

"You can trust *me*, Lara. That's the truth. And you can trust the Passmores, too. In fact, you can trust almost every single person in this house right now. No one here is out to get you."

Lara didn't say anything for a long time. Finally she looked up at him again. "So does this mean things are over between us?"

Jake nodded. "For the time being, yes."

"Well, then that's that." She sniffed loudly and stood up straight. "I guess there's no point in hanging around in here anymore, then, is there?"

"No," Jake quietly agreed. "I guess there isn't."

Aisha was lurking in the corner of the dining room when Christopher finally confronted her.

"We need to talk," he stated. "Right now."

She nodded, feeling light-headed. For a brief moment she thought she would faint. She almost *wished* she would faint—anything to possibly postpone this moment.

"I found an empty room upstairs," he said. "Let's go."

"But it's almost midnight," she argued desperately. "Maybe we should—"

"I don't care, Eesh," he interrupted. "I've waited long enough. I can't wait any longer."

She nodded, silently trailing him through the living room and into the foyer. She could feel the curious stares of Lucas and Kalif upon her as she passed them and headed up the stairs.

They're all wondering what my answer will be. They couldn't possibly imagine that I still have no idea myself.

Christopher turned the corner and gestured to a darkened door across the hall from Nina's room. "In here," he said, standing aside to let her pass first.

Aisha turned the lights on. The room was cozy and romantic, sparsely furnished and softly lit. There was only a desk and a large double bed with a beautiful Colonial-style quilt. As she sat down on it she had a sudden vision of her own house, thirty years from now, with the same little guest room tucked up on the second floor. . . .

Christopher closed the door behind him and stood before her.

This was the man she loved. She stared up at him, so handsome in his dark suit. This was the man of her dreams.

"Christopher," she said, looking straight into his eyes, "I can't marry you."

His face remained impassive. He acknowledged her decision with only the slightest nod.

"I knew you were going to say no," he said after a moment. His voice was oddly calm.

"I didn't even know what I was going to say until just this moment," Aisha said. "Christopher, I love you so much. You have no idea. . . ." She sighed. "I wish I could show you. But I just can't make the commitment—not right now, not at this stage in my life. Do you understand?"

"I understand." He swallowed. "I do."

"This doesn't have to be the end of us," she pleaded. "It doesn't. I'll visit you whenever I have a chance, and you can visit me—"

"Don't try to comfort me, Eesh," he said, raising his hands. "I don't need to be comforted. I have your answer, and that's what I wanted."

Aisha shook her head. "Please say you love me. Please just say it."

"You know how I feel." His voice was beginning to grow strained.

"I'm so sorry—"

"You don't have to apologize. There's just . . . there's just one thing I want to say. I *do* have an idea how much you love me. And it's not enough to be my wife."

He turned and left the room.

Aisha rubbed her eyes. Amazingly enough, no tears would come. Maybe the shock of what had just happened still hadn't fully hit her.

"Everyone!" Mrs. Mendel called excitedly from downstairs. "One minute till midnight! Everyone gather 'round!"

In a state of absolute numbness, Aisha pulled herself off the bed and walked back down to the living room. The rest of the guests had already gathered there. She glanced across the room at Zoey and Lara. They, too, had been crying, she suddenly realized. Her gaze then flickered over the anguished faces of Lucas, Jake, and Christopher.

Nobody got what they wanted tonight.

"Okay," Mrs. Mendel cried from the middle of the throng. She looked at her watch, then raised her hand. Mr. Geiger stood next to her on one side, poised with a bottle of champagne. Claire and Aaron stood on the other side, the only two people her age who looked happy.

"Ten," Mrs. Mendel began. "Nine . . ."

Everyone else took up the chant: "Eight . . . seven . . . six . . . five . . . four . . . three . . . two . . . one . . . happy New Year!"

The cork exploded out of Mr. Geiger's bottle, and the house erupted with cheering.

"Now, people," Mr. Geiger said, once the tumult had died down, "we have a very important announcement to make. Both Sarah and I wanted this to be the very first news of the New Year."

Spontaneous smiles began to spread across the faces of the guests.

Mr. Geiger paused, heightening the suspense. There was a palpable buzz now; the room seemed almost poised to burst.

It was then that Aisha caught a last glimpse of Christopher's sad face. She suddenly knew what the news would be.

Oh, no—please don't say it now. You can't say it now. . . .

Mr. Geiger grabbed Mrs. Mendel's hand and thrust it into the air. "We're getting married!"

New Year's Resolutions: The Girls

Zoey
1) Never lie again
2) Act nicer toward Lara
3) Take an oath of celibacy and avoid boys for the rest of my life

Claire
1) Stop meddling in people's affairs
2) Somehow persuade Aaron to convince his mother to call off the wedding

Nina
1) Stop eating enough chocolate on a weekly basis to fill a small football stadium
2) Listen to Rancid twenty-four hours a day at top volume, eventually driving Claire to throw herself from her widow's walk
3) Somehow convince my father to call off the wedding
4) Sleep with Benjamin as often as possible

Aisha

1) Write Christopher once a day
2) Call Christopher twice a day
3) Visit Christopher as soon as I can afford it

New Year's Resolutions: The Guys

Lucas
1) Study more
2) Hook up with as many girls as I can in order to forget about Zoey

Benjamin
1) Practice the saxophone
2) Act nicer toward Lara
3) Sleep with Nina as often as possible
4) Regain my vision

Jake
1) Quit drinking
2) Study harder and get my homework in on time
3) Not fool around with either Lara or Louise Kronenberger

Christopher
1) Forget about Chatham Island completely and never come back
2) Win the lottery

Claire

I can't really tell if I'm worried about the future. I guess I am. But part of me is very optimistic. For the first time in my life, I feel as if I'm on the right track. I feel as if I can give for the simple pleasure of giving, without expecting some secret benefit in return.

That sounds pretty lame, doesn't it? Well, I'm new at this. I've never felt this way before about anyone. I guess I really am in love. I just hope this doesn't mean I turn into some gushy, servile idiot—like Nina, for instance.

Oh ... maybe that's a little harsh. I am happy for Nina—and Benjamin, too, for that matter. For a long time I was jealous of them, because I never thought I'd experience that closeness or compatibility with anyone myself. I'd never thought I'd find someone so perfectly tailor-made for me—until I met Aaron.

The only problem is that Aaron's mother is marrying my father.

That shouldn't really be a problem, right? I mean, we're not related or anything. We don't share any genetic material. We just happened to be in the right place at the right time.

Or the wrong time, depending on how you look at it.

Aaron used to joke about the possibility of this happening, but now that our parents have formally announced their engagement, I think he's as concerned as I am. Neither of them knows about us. And I really don't know how my father would react. It was bad enough when Benjamin dumped me for Nina, but this is a much stickier situation.

Then again, I'm sure this isn't the first time something like this has happened. (Which reminds me, I still have to read _Emma_.) In a way, it's almost inevitable. I mean, if the parents are so compatible, why shouldn't their children be as well?

Maybe there's some interest group on the Internet that could help me. I wouldn't be surprised. After all, "Kill Jay Leno" worked wonders.

Fifteen

The first three days of the New Year were an absolute blur. Claire spent most of them helping her father and Mrs. Mendel make plans—deciding on the date, the location, and the size of the ceremony. Nina joined by phone when she could. It seemed as if everyone agreed on a few basic details. The wedding had to be on Chatham Island—preferably outside, which meant it had to be during the summer. There had to be a live band. Most important, it had to be *big*.

Finally, on January fourth, the house had once again calmed down enough for Claire to start thinking about the rest of her life—namely, Aaron's departure. It was their last full day together; Aaron was leaving the next morning.

Right after she woke up, Claire hastily dressed and embarked on the cold, half-hour climb up the hill to Gray House. When she arrived, she proceeded directly up the stairs, tiptoeing past Aisha's room. It would be best *not* to stop in and say hello. Claire still hadn't talked to her—or anyone else, for that matter—since the night of the party. But judging from Aisha's teary exit, Claire figured she still needed some time alone. Aisha would let people know when she was ready to talk.

Aaron's door was closed. "Anyone home?" she asked, knocking.

"Come in," he replied.

Claire pushed the door open slowly. Aaron's room was even more of a mess than usual. She realized, with sudden gloom, that he had already begun to pack. Piles of folded clothing were everywhere on the floor. The trunk that had been hidden under the bed was pulled out and opened. Aaron was sitting on his bed in a pair of flannel pajamas, hunched over a crumpled piece of paper.

The shoe box sat next to him.

"Getting an early start on packing?" she asked, trying not to look at it.

"Yeah . . . ," he said after a long while. He was completely engrossed in what he was reading. "My mom has been nagging me."

As much as Claire tried to ignore the shoe box, she couldn't. She knew all about what was inside. All at once she felt guilty, almost unclean. Sneaking into his room while he was out and going through his things had been deplorable. She'd justified the act to herself by a desire to discover the "real" Aaron Mendel. But had the letter from Julia really told her *that* much? Had it told her anything she wouldn't have found out anyway?

She sat down next to him. He instantly folded the paper. Whatever it was, it had been handwritten—by a girl. The large, rounded letters were unmistakably feminine.

"What's that?" she asked.

"Oh, nothing," he said quickly, stuffing it into the shoe box and closing it up. "Just an old letter."

Claire nodded. "Do you save all your old letters?" she asked casually, curious to see if he would reveal the contents of the shoe box to her of his own free will.

"A lot of them," he admitted with a regretful laugh. "I . . . uh . . . keep them to remind myself of the mistakes I've made. It doesn't really seem to work, though."

Claire put her hand on his knee. He couldn't have given a more perfect answer. And this time it wasn't because he was acting or because he wanted to elicit a specific reaction. It was just the simple truth. "I like you," she found herself saying idiotically.

Aaron put his arm around her. He seemed preoccupied, melancholy. "I like you, too."

"What's wrong?" she murmured.

He shrugged. "I'm not too psyched about leaving."

"Well, if it's any consolation, I'm not too psyched, either."

He removed his arm, then tossed the shoe box back into the trunk. "It's funny," he said, shaking his head. "I feel as if I wasted most of my time here."

"Gee, Aaron, thanks a lot," she said, with just a touch of sarcasm.

"No, no—I mean . . . well, that's the whole point," he said slowly. "If I hadn't spent four weeks playing stupid games with you and Zoey, I would have been a lot happier."

I guess you would have, she thought, feeling a strange jumble of hurt, jealousy, and happiness all mixed together. He'd obviously cared for Zoey, but he realized now that he cared more for her. Her plan had been a success after all. "Well, it all ended up working out, right?"

"Yeah. Only now I'm leaving and I won't see you again for six months."

Claire leaned toward him. "I guess that means we

have to make the most of the time we have left," she whispered.

Aaron grinned. "That sounds like something a guy would say."

She cocked an eyebrow suggestively. "You should have figured out by now that I wear the pants in this relationship."

Aaron responded by kissing her. His full, soft lips melded to hers; his hand gently caressed the back of her hair. She could feel his heart beating. It would have been so perfect . . . if he weren't leaving in twenty-four hours.

Finally they drew apart.

"That was nice," she breathed, holding his hand.

"There's more where that came from."

Her eyes began to get misty. For the first time in a long, long while, Claire didn't feel ashamed for getting emotional. "I'm going to miss you so much. . . ."

"We're going to be together again soon," he soothed. "I'm going to try to come visit."

"Aaron—are we going to tell our parents?"

He smiled. "So you've been thinking about that, too, huh?"

"I'm worried my dad will freak out," she mumbled, shaking her head. "I'd hate to make him mad. He's been so happy lately." She snickered. "Almost *too* happy."

"My mom has that effect on people."

Not on me, Claire thought—but she did feel a little guilty for having privately nicknamed Aaron's mother Tattoo. After all, it wasn't Sarah Mendel's fault that she was short.

"Maybe we should just wait," Claire said finally.

Aaron nodded. "And in the meantime we can write

letters." He patted the shoe box. "I need some more reminders of the things I've done *right* in my life."

"So what was it like when the midget and my dad sprang the news?" Nina asked, sucking on an unlit Lucky Strike. She was sprawled out on Zoey's bed, still recovering from the six-hour bus ride and ferry trip back home. Mr. Geiger, Mrs. Mendel, and Zoey had all been waiting for her when she got off the ferry, but she had claimed her butt hurt too much to make the walk all the way back to her own home. Luckily, her dad had been too giddy to argue.

"To tell you the truth, I hardly noticed," Zoey said, sitting at her desk and staring vacantly out the window. "I wasn't exactly in the most attentive state of mind."

"We Geigers really know how to throw a party, huh? One engagement, one refusal to get engaged, one couple formed, and two breakups." She whistled. "Whew. What a night."

"One couple formed?" Zoey turned toward Nina, frowning.

Nina nodded. "Aaron and Claire, remember? *You* told me about that one."

"Oh. Yeah. Them." Zoey's face drooped slightly. She turned back to the window.

"They're perfect for each other, Zoey," Nina said quickly. She still couldn't believe that Zoey had actually *liked* that guy, but she felt bad. "They're Mr. and Mrs. I-look-really-good-but-inside-I'm-a-twisted-monster."

"Can we please talk about something else?" Zoey grumbled.

"Well . . . what else is there to talk about?"

"How about college applications?" Zoey shuffled some papers on her desk, then picked up a form. It looked as if it had been completed; Nina could see a neatly written essay. She chuckled to herself. It figured Zoey would already have her applications done.

"How would you answer this one?" Zoey asked. " 'Describe in one paragraph an episode that you regret.' "

"Not entering the Miss America contest." Nina blew an imaginary smoke ring. "I was a shoo-in this year."

"Seriously, Nina. How would you answer that?"

"What do I regret? Jeez, what kind of college asks a question like that? Are you applying to seminary school or something?"

"Just answer the question," Zoey insisted.

Nina thought for a minute. She was surprised to find that there actually wasn't a whole lot that she regretted. Well, aside from the obvious—like going to stay with her sleazebag uncle that summer. But other than that, she'd been pretty happy with the way she'd led her life.

"Letting Benjamin talk me into coming home before he got his bandages off," she said finally. "I mean, I might as well have come home for New Year's Eve. I actually *do* kind of regret missing that party."

"Oh, yeah," Zoey said flatly. She dropped the application form back on her desk. "I forgot you have a morbid fascination with watching all of your dearest friends suffer."

Nina sat up straight. "Look, you may be bummed out now, but I seriously think this is the best thing that could have happened to all parties involved."

"What?" Zoey cried.

"I mean it." Nina thrust her arm toward the window. "It will finally force you snobby Chatham Island girls to look to the mainland for your boyfriends."

"Us 'snobby Chatham Island girls'?" Zoey shook

her head, but she was grinning. "Look who's talking."

"It was an extraordinary fluke that I happened to find my boyfriend here," Nina said, sucking on her cigarette. "The odds against it are so high. Such a phenomenon can't be repeated more than once."

Zoey's grin slowly vanished. "Maybe you're right," she said with a sigh.

"I'm sure I am," Nina stated confidently. "Besides, it's bad for the gene pool if people don't get off the island. Our great-grandchildren will all end up looking like those people in *Deliverance*—you know, all pale and deformed, with big yellow buck teeth." She paused, then added quietly, "Who knows—maybe I'll have to end up looking to the mainland, too."

Zoey's eyes widened. "What are you saying?"

"What I'm *saying* is . . ." Nina looked away. "I don't know if Benjamin will want to go out with me when he sees what I really look like." The sentence tumbled out of her mouth in one breath, as if it were one long word.

Zoey burst out laughing.

Nina glared at her. "What?"

"Nina, that's the dumbest—"

"Your eyes have gotten used to me," Nina interrupted. "I'm being completely serious now, Zoey." She pulled the cigarette out of her mouth and gestured at herself with it. Not only did she *feel* totally slimy after having been on the bus all morning, but she knew she looked like an absolute slob. Her fatigues were smudged with food stains. Her greasy brown hair was hanging in her eyes. And her belly, thanks to all shc'd eaten over Christmas, looked even bigger than it had the last time she'd examined it.

"Just *look* at me!" she wailed.

"I am looking at you," Zoey replied. "And I'm not turning to stone."

Nina just shook her head. "Give it some time," she mumbled. "The petrification process takes a few minutes."

"Nina, you're being stupid. First of all, Benjamin *loves* you. You could look like a baboon for all he cares, and that will be true even when he gets his vision back. Second of all, you're *attractive*. Believe me, I know you well enough to tell you otherwise if I thought so."

"And I know *you* well enough to know that that's complete BS," Nina said.

"Oh, yeah?" A tired little laugh escaped Zoey's lips. "Just go ask Lara. She'll tell you."

Nina wrinkled her nose. "What did you say to Lara?"

"I told her she was ugly."

"You *what*?" She started laughing. That was the most ludicrous thing she had ever heard.

"It's not funny, Nina. Look, never mind." Zoey pulled her desk chair toward the bed and leaned forward. "The point is, you're not ugly. So stop feeling sorry for yourself."

"I'm not feeling sorry for myself," she moped. "I'm just . . . feeling sorry for myself."

"Well, why don't you go home and take a shower or something?" Zoey suggested. "Or clean your fingernails for once. Or try another shade of lipstick besides purple. . . ." Her voice gradually grew softer and softer until it faded altogether. Suddenly she sat up straight, grinning like a person who had just gone insane.

"Uh-oh." Nina eyed Zoey distrustfully. "I don't like that look on your face."

Zoey bolted up from the chair. "I have a brilliant idea. Come on."

"Where are we going?"

"We're going over to Eesh's," Zoey announced. "She and I are going to rebuild Nina Geiger. We have the technology."

Nina began shaking her head. "Zoey—"

"Come *on*." Zoey grabbed her arm and yanked her off the bed. "You said you wanted some help. Well, I'm going to help you."

Nina was beginning to feel sick. "I take it back," she said. "I think I'm gorgeous."

"I'm not taking no for an answer," Zoey said adamantly. "You, my friend, are about to get the makeover of a lifetime."

LUCAS

Sure, I'm worried about the future. I'm worried that every single college admissions officer is going to look at my record and say, "I see here that your extracurricular activities include two years behind bars. Well, thanks for applying, anyway. Don't trip on your way out."

I'm also worried that once I'm rejected by every college in the country, my father will declare once again that I'm not fit to be his son and then ship me off to Texas. That wouldn't surprise me in the least. He's already made it pretty clear he thinks I'm worthless.

But the thing that worries me the most is that I'll never find another girlfriend like Zoey. For a while there I was literally embarrassed about how much I loved her. There were a few glorious months when I felt like the luckiest guy on earth.

Then, of course, everything got confused and complicated and eventually ruined.

So no, I'm not too hopeful about the future.

Sixteen

Lucas stood on the edge of the back deck of his house, leaning listlessly over the railing and staring down at the Passmores' little kitchen. He pulled his black wool cap over his ears. The early afternoon sun was bright enough to warm him slightly, but the winter wind whipped at his face. In the Passmores' kitchen, Lara sat with her back to him, reading the paper. Zoey was nowhere to be seen. Four days had passed since he had last spoken to her. He hadn't gone that long without speaking to her since he'd gotten out of YA.

It suddenly occurred to him that he didn't even know where she was right then.

Things really are *over between us.*

The sliding door opened, and Lucas turned to see his father poking his head out. "Lucas, I need you to run an errand for me," he said.

Sighing, Lucas pushed himself off the railing and walked back into the kitchen. "What is it?"

"We're out of nails," Lucas's father said, closing the door behind them.

Lucas rolled his eyes. "And you need them right now?"

"Yes, I do," Mr. Cabral barked. "Not everyone's

on vacation. Some of us actually have some work to do—''

"Fine, fine," Lucas interrupted. "I'll go."

Mr. Cabral headed for the basement stairs. "That grocery store on Sheffield sells them."

"I *know*, Dad," Lucas answered, watching his father plod down the steps. "Um—aren't you forgetting something? Like money?"

"I'll pay you back later," he called.

Typical, Lucas thought with a snort. For a moment he was very tempted to just go upstairs and forget about the stupid errand. But there was no point in making a bad situation worse; he'd just end up paying for it later. He reached into his pocket to see if he had any cash.

His fingers brushed something unfamiliar: something slick and new and smooth.

Then he remembered.

That morning he'd transferred all his money and cards to Zoey's wallet.

He still wasn't sure why he'd done that. Maybe he'd thought he'd be getting back at her somehow by actually using the wallet for its intended purpose—especially after the way she'd hurled it at him in a fit of jealous rage. But as he pulled it out and stared at it, he felt only a dull ache in his stomach. He'd made a mistake. Using the wallet simply wasn't worth the pain of being reminded of Zoey day in and day out, every time he reached into his pocket.

"Lucas, are you still here?" his father yelled.

"I'm leaving, I'm leaving." Lucas marched through the hall and slammed the front door behind him.

Maybe I should just use this opportunity to get rid of the wallet right now, he thought as he rounded the corner onto Center Street. Yes—it would be perfect. He would drop by Zoey's house and hand it to her.

Thanks, he would say, but he really didn't need it. And if she wasn't there, all the better. He would just leave it on her desk.

Picking up his pace, he turned left on South and then left again on Camden. His footsteps scraped on the gravel as he approached the door.

For an instant he hesitated. His heart bumped loudly in his chest. Why was he so nervous? He was angry—angry at her, angry at his father, angry at the world. There was no reason to be nervous. He rang the doorbell.

A moment later Lara opened the door.

"Hey, what's up?" Lucas asked.

"Oh, not much." She smiled. "I'm just getting ready to move out."

"Oh." He tried to smile back, but his lips felt strained. "Is, uh, Zoey around?"

Lara shook her head. "She left with Nina about an hour ago."

"Can I come in? I just need to drop something off."

"Sure," she said, stepping aside. "Do whatever you want. It's not *my* house."

Lucas closed the door carefully behind him, watching with a little shiver as she disappeared back into the kitchen. The girl had given him the willies ever since that night at Jake's. The Passmores were seriously lucky to be getting rid of her. Christopher was right: She was bad news.

He headed up the stairs and opened the door, for what he realized would probably be the last time, on the familiar world of Zoey's room.

Before he even stepped inside, he took a few moments to soak up everything with his eyes: the little desk by the dormer, the bureau, the cozy bed. The room even *smelled* of Zoey—soft and sweet. He felt dizzy, cotton-mouthed. He had a lot of good memories centered around that room. That was worth something, wasn't it?

There was no point in sticking around. He fished the wallet out of his pants with trembling, sweaty fingers and removed the cards and money. Then he shoved the contents into his front pocket and tossed the wallet onto the desk.

It landed next to Mr. Passmore's old typewriter, which Zoey had brought up to her room for some reason.

He took a step forward, squinting at a piece of paper lying next to the machine. It was a college application form, upon which Zoey had typed a short paragraph. The instructions at the top read:

Describe in one paragraph an episode
that you regret:

Lucas swallowed. His eyes flashed down the page.

The episode I regret most in my life
happened only very recently. I
destroyed a close relationship—one
that I value more than any outside my
own family. The person with whom I'd had
this relationship embodies all of the
traits I admire most in a person:
honesty, loyalty, sensitivity, and at
the same time a strong desire to improve
himself. Yet this person is also a
pessimist and a cynic. These aspects of
his personality are the result of his
having been unjustly incarcerated for
two years. I consider myself an

optimist, and I tried my best to help
him overcome this negative experience.
Just when he had finally started to put
the past behind him, I betrayed him. I
·regret the betrayal, but I regret far
more that I may have destroyed his
ability to hope and to trust in
others.

Lucas read the paragraph again, then again. *"Destroyed his ability to hope and to trust in others."* He
slumped down in Zoey's chair and struggled to process
the words. Had she done that to him? Perhaps she
had—but he hadn't really thought about it, at least not
in such stark terms. All he'd thought about was getting
back at her.

But Zoey's mind didn't work that way. She never
thought of revenge. In spite of everything he'd done to
her, she'd written that he was honest, loyal, and sen-
sitive. She'd written her college essay about *him.*

Was he even worth the space on her application
form? If the essay would help her get into college,
maybe he was. But there was no doubt in his mind that
what she'd written would do exactly that. Nobody expressed herself as well as Zoey. She deserved to get
into any college she wanted. She deserved the best.

Lucas found he was shaking. Never in a million
years could he write an essay like that. How could she
still feel that way about him? She was so smart, so
articulate, so talented. No wonder she'd been attracted
to Aaron Mendel. He was all of those things, too. But
Lucas Cabral was . . . what? An ex-convict. A mediocre
student. A self-centered jerk.

He snatched the empty wallet off the desk and stared

at it. Was he even worthy of this gift? No—not now, not ever. He cringed, thinking of the way he'd acted toward Zoey on New Year's Eve. Her brother was in the hospital, her half sister was making her life a living hell—and Lucas Cabral had stepped right in for the knockout punch, telling her, in essence, that she should cry about her problems to someone else. And yet according to the essay, he was supposed to embody loyalty and sensitivity. How could she have written those words?

But she had. *She* had seen something in him—something he certainly couldn't see himself. Maybe he still had a chance. After all, she'd written about his qualities in the present tense. Evidently she still valued their relationship. But valuing someone differed from loving someone. Did she still love him?

Lucas leaped out of the chair. If she didn't love him, he knew the essay would prove true. He *would* lose whatever hope he had left.

"Okay, Nina," Aisha said, carefully cutting away one last strand of hair. "Are you ready?"

"Ready as I'll ever be," Nina mumbled.

Aisha stepped back and scrutinized Nina from top to bottom. The transformation was truly radical. Aisha had lent Nina a flowery print dress and had cut her hair into a cute little bob that perfectly complemented her roundish face. But that was only the start. Gone were the combat boots, the filthy pants, the dirt-encrusted fingernails, and the purple lipstick. A touch of eyeliner accentuated the gray of her eyes. There was no doubt about it: Nina was stunning.

"I don't know why you made me do this," Nina said as Zoey excitedly unfastened the sheet they'd wrapped around her to catch the hair. "I felt fine before."

"Oh, you'll see," Aisha said, unable to keep from smiling. The excitement was contagious. Even Nina was starting to grin in anticipation.

At first, when Zoey and Nina had shown up uninvited at her door, Aisha had just wanted them to get lost. But the more she'd worked on Nina, the better she'd felt. They'd been slaving away in the lavish bathroom of the Governor's Room—the biggest guest room in the house—for over two hours. She'd even managed to forget about Christopher once or twice.

"Here goes," Zoey said. She swiveled Nina's chair around on the floor and pointed her in the direction of the full-length mirror on the back of the door.

Nina's eyes bulged.

"Well?" Zoey asked, beaming at Aisha.

"I—I—" Nina stuttered, slack-jawed.

"Now here's a woman no man will be able to resist," Aisha said.

Nina slowly stood and stared at herself, turning one way and then the other. She shook her head. "I didn't think it was possible," she said. "I mean, I've always thought that makeovers are the lamest thing in the world. I still believe that."

"Hey!" Zoey cried, punching her.

"No, seriously—thanks, you guys." Nina fell back into the chair and looked at them. "Now all I have to do is lose fifteen pounds."

"Nina, you are *not* fat," Aisha scolded. "Stop it."

"I'm fatter than *you*," Nina retorted, running her hands curiously through her newly styled hair.

"Doesn't count," Zoey said. "Eesh is abnormally sticklike." She gently removed Nina's hands from the top of her head. "Now leave your hair alone. You don't want to ruin all our hard work."

"*My* hard work, Zo," Aisha said, snapping her scissors at her. "After all, you just advised."

Zoey proudly gestured toward Nina's hair. "Great advice, wouldn't you say?"

Aisha nodded. "Benjamin is gonna flip when he sees you."

"Oh, this is just so much fun!" Nina suddenly cried, clapping her feet on the floor. "I feel so *girly*." She stuck her finger in her mouth and hunched over in a very graphic impression of self-induced vomiting.

"First time feeling like a girl, huh?" Zoey teased. "Hey, maybe you'll like it."

"You *are* a girl, after all," Aisha reminded her.

"I *am*?" Nina frowned. "No wonder I have so much trouble going to the bathroom standing up."

"Yuck," Aisha muttered. She bent down and began gathering the hair-covered sheet off the floor.

All of a sudden there was a knock on the door.

"Who is it?" Aisha asked. It was probably her mother, coming to nag them to start cleaning up.

"Christopher."

Aisha dropped the sheet. The blood instantly drained from her face.

"I can come back later if this is a bad time," he said.

"No, no—we were just leaving," Nina said before Aisha could even reply. Nina jumped out of the chair and opened the door, with Zoey close on her heels.

Christopher grinned slightly as the two of them hurried past him. "Wow, Nina—I almost didn't recognize you."

"That's the point," Nina's disembodied voice called. She was already scampering down the stairs

148

with Zoey. "I've been recruited by the CIA, and this is my disguise."

A moment later the front door slammed.

Christopher laughed, shaking his head. "Man," he said after a moment. "That girl is crazy."

Aisha remained immobile, unable to do anything but stare at him.

"So, look," he said, avoiding her eyes. His expression grew serious. "I just wanted to drop off the car you gave me. It's right out front. I don't think I'll be needing it anymore."

"I . . . I don't want it," Aisha murmured.

Christopher shrugged. "Well, I bet you can sell it. I'll see you around, all right? Take it easy." He turned to leave.

"Christopher—wait!" Aisha dashed out of the bathroom and threw her arms around him.

He remained perfectly rigid.

"Christopher, please," she whispered. "I can't let you go like this."

"I don't know what to tell you." His voice wasn't harsh; it was simply colorless, lacking in any emotion. "It's not my problem."

"You know that's not true." She stepped away. "I know you still care for me. I know it."

He shook his head noncommittally. "Think what you want to think."

She swallowed. "I'm not going to cry right now," she said in a tight voice. "I've cried enough already. I just want to promise you . . . that I'm going to write to you every day, and—"

"Save it, Eesh," he snapped. "Look, don't waste your time and energy writing to me. I'm not going to write you back."

Aisha shook her head. "I don't believe that," she

pronounced. "You're angry now, so you're saying a lot of things you don't mean."

"Wise up, all right?" His eyes were fiery. "It's *over,* okay? The end. Period. Don't patronize me by telling me you're going to keep in touch. It's insulting."

"It's over?" she repeated, hanging on to the one phrase that was now echoing in her mind.

"That's right, Eesh. You're finally catching on." He paused. "Good luck getting into college, okay? I hope you get what you're after. And tell your parents I appreciate everything they did for me."

Aisha nodded. She couldn't bring herself to look at him anymore. "Good-bye, Christopher. I . . . I love you. And I always will."

"You'll get over it, Eesh. You're halfway there."

There was the briefest instant of hesitation. Then he exited the room and Aisha's life.

Seventeen

Jake sat at his desk, wondering if every Saturday night for the rest of his life was going to be as dull as this one. He'd been poring over his college application forms for the past few hours, and he'd still gotten absolutely nowhere. The questions were all so *intimidating*. Just looking at them made him feel like the most uninvolved, unmotivated, uninspired student on the planet.

He picked up one of the sheets: *List any extracurricular activities: clubs, student government, volunteer organizations, etc.*

Aside from football and baseball, he wasn't involved in any extracurricular activities. Well, that wasn't quite true. He belonged to Alcoholics Anonymous. But that wasn't exactly the kind of after-school activity colleges were looking for in their prospective students.

Jake leaned back in his chair and thought for a minute. He *had* to be involved in some other club or organization, right? After all, he went to church occasionally. That probably counted for something. He *volunteered* to go to church. Maybe he could even exaggerate that somehow—

A light tap on the sliding glass door interrupted his thoughts.

Oh, no.

There was only one person who would show up unannounced on a Saturday night. She'd done it once before.

He pushed himself out of his chair, feeling a wave of apprehension. *Why does she have to come here now? Didn't she get the message at the party?*

"Hi, Lara," he said as he slid the door open.

Sure enough, she scurried in and yanked the door closed behind her, rubbing herself with her hands. "Brrrr. It's cold out there."

"What are you doing here?" he asked.

She sat down on his bed and swung her backpack off her shoulder. "I, uh . . . wanted to give you something," she said. "It's a present."

Jake shook his head. Anger swelled within him. He felt as if he were experiencing déjà vu. He knew all too well about Lara's unexpected "gifts."

"It's not what you think, Jake." She unzipped her bag.

"Lara, I told you, I—"

But before he could finish, she pulled out a small canvas. It was no bigger than a piece of notebook paper, but on it had been painted an extraordinary likeness of his own face. Jake's jaw dropped.

"Do you like it?" she asked, holding it up for him to see.

Jake was speechless. "You . . . you did that?" he finally asked, dumbfounded.

"Mmm-hmmm." She nodded, handing it to him. "I've been working on it for the past few days. It felt good to paint again. I haven't done it in a while."

Jake studied it for a few seconds. He couldn't believe the detail. Every feature had been perfectly captured—his jaw, his hair, his eyes, everything. But there was something more. He was smiling in the painting. He never smiled when he looked in the mirror. He'd seen himself smile only in photographs, and he had never thought that he looked nice in those photos, the way he did in Lara's painting. It wasn't that the painting made him look nice in the sense of being attractive; it made him look . . . kind.

"Do you like it?" she asked.

"Yeah, yeah—it's great," he said, nodding emphatically. "Thanks a lot, Lara."

She shrugged. "No problem."

He sat back down in his chair and placed the painting delicately on top of the desk, then looked at her, still stunned. "Why'd you *do* it?" he asked.

"Why'd I *do* it?" She laughed. "I, uh, really don't know. I guess I was inspired."

"I don't know what to say," Jake mumbled, embarrassed.

"Well, I'm glad you like it." She pulled her knapsack back on and stood up. "I'm sorry I barged in on you like this—I was just worried your dad would answer the phone. I don't think I'm his favorite friend of yours at the moment."

Jake shook his head. "Lara—"

"Don't." She held out her hands. "Come on, Jake, you don't need to say anything. I made this because I wanted to. You don't owe me anything. You've already given me way too much." She smiled demurely. "Just look at it as a little token of my thanks."

"I'm going to put it up right now," he said.

"Good." She nodded, looking satisfied. "Well, look, I gotta go back to the Passmores' and finish packing. I'll give you a call in a couple of days, okay?" She pulled the door open and gave him one last solemn little grin. "Maybe I'll even come to one of those meetings with you."

The door shut behind her, and she was gone.

Jake sighed deeply. He turned and looked once again at Lara's painting. It really was remarkable. He'd never known she was so talented. Of course, she'd never talked about her paintings to him. And the ones he'd seen had been strange and abstract, beyond his understanding.

He smiled, feeling somewhat pitiful. Maybe that was why she'd given him a painting that was so true to life, so *obvious*. His small brain wasn't capable of grasping anything more complex.

But he was making progress; he knew that. He'd learned that the line between right and wrong was never clearly defined—and that was a pretty big, difficult step for him. After all, he'd managed to forgive Lucas. He'd even found that he *liked* Lucas. And at the same time, he knew that part of him would never forgive Lucas for that night two and a half long years ago.

Nobody was all bad. Even the people in AA weren't all bad, although many of them had done terrible things. Lara wasn't all bad, either. No, Lara was a very confused, very bright girl who had never had a decent relationship in her whole life. Her problems weren't due to the fact that she was a mean-spirited person. They were due to the fact that deep down she was a good person struggling to break out of her hard, self-imposed shell.

The application forms spread out on his desk demanded his attention, but Jake knew his concentration had been totally shot. He couldn't decide what he was feeling just then—a little regret, a little guilt, but at the same time a peculiar sort of happiness.

He got up from his chair and moved to his bed to

stretch out for a little while. He paused when he saw something on the mattress. It was a little blue cloth purse with a zipper. It must have fallen out of Lara's bag when she'd gotten up to leave.

He leaned forward to pick it up. The purse made a swishing noise. He instantly felt ill. There was a small, flat bottle inside.

His fingers shook as he unzipped the little zipper and removed the bottle. It was a flask of that cheap tequila Lara loved so much. It had been barely touched. On the side of the bottle, Lara had taped a note to herself: *Save for your last night at the Passmores' house. Enjoy it, McAvoy! It will be your last.*

For a moment Jake wondered if she had deliberately left it there, to prove to him in a very bizarre manner that she was serious about quitting drinking. It wouldn't surprise him; nothing about her could surprise him anymore. But even if she had, it really didn't matter. Jake had the bottle now, and she didn't.

"Jake!" his father called from upstairs. "What are you up to?"

"Working on my applications, Dad," he called, staring at the bottle.

"Did somebody just stop by?"

"Yeah. Lara. She wanted to drop off a painting she made for me."

"A *what*?"

"A painting. Come down and take a look."

As his father came downstairs Jake walked out into the bitter cold and poured the liquor off the terrace, watching it vanish into the black night.

Then he went back inside and showed his father the painting.

Eighteen

"Benjamin?" Dr. Martin was asking. "Benjamin, are you awake?"

Benjamin slowly became aware that someone was gently shaking his arm. He yawned and stretched, trying to snap out of his drowsy stupor.

"How'd you sleep?" Dr. Martin asked.

"Uh, okay, I guess," Benjamin mumbled hoarsely. He thought for a minute. He'd had a lot of trouble falling asleep because he was so nervous, but he must have finally managed to doze off for good in the middle of the night. "I don't think I slept as much as I would have liked," he added.

"Well, that's to be expected," Dr. Martin said. "You have a big morning ahead of you."

Benjamin nodded, now fully awake. His heart was already beating faster than usual. Normally he was hungry in the morning, but right then he couldn't even think about food. He pushed himself up in bed.

"If it's okay with you," Dr. Martin said, "we'd like to remove the bandages first thing."

"That's fine with me." Benjamin nodded vigorously. "Is my mom around?"

"She's already waiting for you in the treatment

room. I'm going to take you there in a minute. I just want to check a few things first. Would you lie back down flat, please?"

Benjamin quickly lay down. *Today's the day*. He still couldn't quite believe it.

"So you must be pretty excited about getting out of this place," Dr. Martin said dryly. He leaned over Benjamin's head and placed his fingers on Benjamin's temples.

"Uh, yeah, I guess I am."

"I won't take offense." Dr. Martin moved his fingers across Benjamin's forehead and applied some pressure. "Even I have to admit the food here is pretty bad. How does that feel?"

"Fine," Benjamin replied, feeling very relieved. Even the day before, his head had hurt a little when Dr. Martin examined him—but now there was no pain whatsoever. It even felt *good*. He almost felt as if he were getting a head massage.

"Well, I think we're all ready, then." Dr. Martin removed his hands. "Let's get going."

Someone else came into the room. Benjamin felt his mattress jerk slightly as someone pulled a lever near the foot of the bed. The next thing he knew, he was rolling out the door.

"So when are you supposed to go back to school?" Dr. Martin asked casually.

"Uh . . . today's Sunday, right?" Benjamin wondered out loud. He had genuinely begun to lose track of the days of the week; his waking hours were all so undifferentiated and monotonous. "Christmas break ends tomorrow, actually."

Dr. Martin chuckled. "Oh, boy. I'm sorry you missed out on your vacation."

"I'm not," Benjamin said. He felt the bed turn to

the left. "Anyway, I would have done the exact same thing at home—lie around and listen to music."

"And spend time with Ms. Geiger?" Dr. Martin suggested.

Benjamin smiled. "That, too."

"You two make a cute couple. I was half tempted to suggest to Nina that she become a doctor. She has a terrific bedside manner."

"Yeah—if you like crude jokes." Benjamin laughed. "I was worried she might have offended some people."

The bed came to a stop, then turned to the right.

"Here we are," Dr. Martin said quietly.

Benjamin felt a soft hand against his.

"What's up, kiddo?" his mother asked.

"Not much." As much as it surprised him, Benjamin no longer felt overly anxious. Dr. Martin's soothing, mindless chatter had almost had the same effect on him as an anesthetic. "I'm ready to get this over with."

"I love you," Mrs. Passmore whispered. She kissed his cheek, gave his hand one last squeeze, then stepped aside.

"Benjamin, before we start, I'd just like to thank you once again for your cooperation," Dr. Martin said. "I couldn't have asked for a better subject. You should feel proud of yourself."

Benjamin paused, waiting for Dr. Martin to add something else, such as "Thanks to you, blind people everywhere will see now" or "Now I really know that we have the capability to restore vision." But he didn't. And Benjamin knew the reason. Dr. Martin still didn't know if the operation had worked.

"Uh, thanks," Benjamin finally said. He swallowed.

"Now just lean back and relax. . . ."

Benjamin's breath was coming in short gasps. He felt a cold sliver of metal brush his cheek and then heard a loud *snip, snip, snip*. The gauze around his head began to loosen. Finally it fell free altogether. But there were still two separate pads covering his eyes. He hadn't even noticed them before.

Dr. Martin gently lifted his head and pulled the gauze out from under it.

"Now, Benjamin," he said, "when I remove the last covering, you may experience an unpleasant sensation. That's the glare of the lights in here, and it's to be expected. Don't be surprised if objects are extremely fuzzy and out of focus. For a while you may not be able to see anything except a harsh white light."

Benjamin nodded. His heart was pounding like a jackhammer.

"Keep both eyes closed until both bandages are off completely," Dr. Martin instructed.

Benjamin held his breath. Dr. Martin peeled away the first pad. The adhesive tape took some of Benjamin's eyebrow with it, but Benjamin was oblivious to the pain, as he was when the second pad was removed.

"You may open your eyes now."

Benjamin waited for a few seconds. This was the moment. His life would never be the same again. He silently said good-bye to the old Benjamin Passmore, then exhaled.

His eyelids fluttered.

For an instant Benjamin caught a glimpse of a dazzling, formless white light.

But almost as soon as the image had registered, it began to dim, like the end of a song fading into silence. He blinked, again and again. But the light was gone. Once more there was only that familiar, enveloping curtain of darkness.

"Benjamin?" he heard his mother ask.

The light was gone.

"It didn't work." His voice seemed to belong to another person. "It didn't work...."

Nineteen

Claire was waiting for Aaron in the living room when he pulled up in Mrs. Mendel's island car. She immediately dashed outside to meet him.

"Hop in," he called, rolling down the window.

Claire squinted into the car. Mrs. Mendel was nowhere to be seen. The backseat was stuffed with Aaron's belongings. "Where's your mom?" Claire asked as she hopped in front.

"She said good-bye to me up at the bed-and-breakfast. I told her I wanted to say good-bye to you on my own."

Claire's eyes widened. "You didn't tell her about—"

"I told her that we'd become close," Aaron said very straightforwardly, roaring down Lighthouse Road in the direction of the ferry. He shrugged, keeping both hands on the wheel. "I don't know what she inferred from that. But she agreed to let us have this time alone together. I told her you'd return the car to her after the ferry left."

"Uh-oh," Claire groaned.

"They're bound to find out sooner or later, Claire."

She glanced at him. She could just see the trace of a grin on his face. Of course. Aaron had aroused his

161

mother's curiosity—leaving Claire to explain everything once *he* was safely far away at boarding school.

"Nice one, Aaron," she said.

"What do you mean?" he asked, pretending to be surprised—but he was laughing.

She smiled. "You always get your way, don't you?"

"Well, yes."

Claire swatted his shoulder. "You'd better watch it. I might have to come to your school and teach you a lesson."

"Now you're talking. No, really—that would be so cool. I'm going to tell all my friends that I'm going out with this amazingly beautiful, incredibly sophisticated girl from a small island in Maine that they've never heard of. They'll think I'm lying, of course—and then you'll show up, and they'll worship me." He slowed the car and pulled to a stop in front of Passmores'.

"So I'm some kind of trophy to you?" Claire teased, but she was flattered. That was the first time Aaron had ever said the words "going out with." It was official.

"Of course you are," Aaron said, leaning back in his seat and looking at her. "A girl like you comes along only once every ten thousand years. You *are* a prize, you know."

Claire just smiled stupidly, unable to respond. She'd never had that problem with anyone before; she'd always had a fast comeback. It was a little disturbing.

"What are you thinking?" Aaron asked.

"I'm thinking that you have this really weird effect on me, and I'm not sure how to react."

Aaron leaned over and caressed her face. "I can think of a way for you to react. . . ."

"Wait, wait," she said, taking his hand from her

cheek and clasping it firmly between her own hands. "I want to talk. The ferry will be here any minute."

Aaron looked over her shoulder in the direction of the landing. "I don't see it."

"Seriously, Aaron."

He looked into her eyes. "Okay. Shoot."

There was no point in hedging. "Are you going to stay faithful to me at boarding school?" she asked.

Aaron sucked in his cheeks thoughtfully, then nodded. "I'm going to try. I really am."

"Try?" she asked doubtfully.

"No." He nodded. "I *will* stay faithful to you. I promise."

"There aren't any cute little preppy girls down there named Binky just waiting to hop in the sack with you?"

"Binky?" Aaron laughed. "No. Muffy, maybe, but definitely not Binky."

"Aaron!"

He put his other hand on top of hers. "Believe me, Claire, no girl at boarding school even comes *close* to you. I wasn't interested in any of them before I left to come here, and I sure won't be now."

"Okay." She nodded.

"Now, back to the subject at hand. . . ." He leaned forward again.

"One more question." Claire backed away from him.

He rolled his eyes. "Yes?"

"Did you say good-bye to Zoey?"

He hesitated, looking away for a second. "I left her a message yesterday," he admitted. "I was actually kind of glad I didn't have to talk to her."

Well, that was fine—but Claire wanted to know more. "What did you say in your message?"

163

He shrugged. "I told her that I was sorry about everything that happened between us, and that in the end she was better off with Lucas. *And* that I was much better off with you." He drew in his breath. "I also told her I hoped everything worked out with Benjamin."

I hope so, too, Claire thought. Poor Zoey. Her life was such a mess at the moment. Claire doubted she would ever get back together with Lucas, not after everything that had happened. And who knew what was going to happen with Benjamin? At least Lara was moving out. "Were you nice?" she asked after a minute.

"I tried to be." Suddenly he pulled his hands away. "There's the ferry."

Claire turned around in her seat just as the ferry's horn blew. She could see the boat now, drifting slowly around the bend toward the dock.

"So much for a long, romantic good-bye," Aaron muttered, hopping out and pulling his bags from the backseat.

"Where's your trunk?" Claire asked curiously. She opened the door and got out to help him, but he'd already slung everything over his shoulders.

"I'm keeping it here," he said. His back bent forward under the weight of his belongings. "This is my new home now, you know," he added with a smile.

Claire nodded. She bit down hard on the inside of her cheek in a vain effort to keep from crying. "Do you, uh, need any help?"

"No, I've got it."

She felt his hand under her chin. He lifted her face and kissed her lightly on the lips.

"Bye, Claire," he murmured.

"I'm going to miss you."

"I'm going to write to you as soon as I get to school." He gave her one last kiss and started walking toward the dock.

"I love you," she blurted.

He stopped and looked over his shoulder. "I love you, too." He blew a doleful kiss at her, then boarded the ferry for Weymouth.

Twenty

"Well, I guess that's about it, Lara," Mr. Passmore said, putting his arm around Zoey's shoulder. "Good luck."

"Thanks." Lara smiled at Zoey. "Thanks for all your help."

Zoey just nodded, unsure of what to say. She stood in the doorway with her dad and took one last look around the barren octagonal room, piled with boxes and unopened suitcases. Christopher had left nothing behind but a bare mattress. Well, that wasn't quite true. He'd also left a hastily scrawled note.

To the Passmores—thanks so much for everything. I don't know what I would have done without you. Working at your restaurant was probably the best job I ever had. I'm not kidding. I'm going to miss you guys a lot. Let me know how Benjamin's operation turns out. I'm sorry I couldn't say good-bye in person, but I still need to pack, and I have to catch the 7:40 ferry.

I'LL WRITE TO YOU ALL AS SOON AS I KNOW
WHERE YOU CAN WRITE ME BACK.

LOVE,
CHRISTOPHER

Zoey still couldn't believe that he had just *fled*—just bolted from the island without even stopping to say good-bye to anyone face-to-face. That wasn't like Christopher; it seemed almost cowardly. But she knew he had his reasons. Chatham Island represented a lot of pain for him. It would take him a long time to get over the memories. He'd probably just wanted to make a clean break.

"I'll see you tomorrow at work, okay?" Mr. Passmore said.

"I'll be there," Lara replied.

"Bye, Lara," Zoey murmured.

"Bye." Lara closed the door gently.

Zoey and Mr. Passmore walked from the old Victorian mansion-turned-apartment-house in silence. Finally, after they were already puttering down Leeward Drive toward home, Mr. Passmore said, "Well, that wasn't so bad, was it?"

Zoey shook her head. "It wasn't bad at all." She stared out the window at Jake's house as they passed it on the right, wondering briefly how he was managing with Alcoholics Anonymous. She hoped Lara would join him there. Neither of them needed any more sadness or confusion in their lives.

Mr. Passmore nodded. "I think everything is going to work out for the best."

"I hope so," Zoey agreed—and she wasn't thinking just of Lara. She hoped everything would work out for Jake, too, and for Christopher—even for Aaron and the soon-to-be-expanded Geiger family, for that matter.

And most especially for Benjamin.

"Aren't you glad I decided to take the day off?" Mr. Passmore asked as he turned right onto South Street. "We can just bum around and do nothing." He laughed. "Just like the good old days."

"Actually, I have to work on my applications—" Zoey broke off when they turned right onto Camden.

Nina and Lucas were sitting outside the front door of the Passmores' house. Zoey gasped. Nina was crying. Lucas had his arm around her.

Zoey leaped out of the car even before Mr. Passmore had come to a complete stop.

"What's wrong?" she asked, rushing over to Nina's side.

"Benjamin," Nina sobbed. "He . . . didn't . . . the operation didn't work. He's still . . ."

Zoey threw her arms around her and hugged Nina as tightly as she could. "Nina, it's going to be okay," she murmured. But her words were comfortless, to Nina as well as to herself.

Mr. Passmore stood over them, his face ashen. "He called you this morning?" he asked.

Nina nodded, wiping her eyes. "He sounded so sad. . . ."

"Come here, Nina." Mr. Passmore opened the door and gently picked her off the ground, leading her inside. "We knew this was a possibility. We have to stay strong. . . ."

The door closed behind them.

Zoey sat for a moment, reeling with the effort to swallow the news. She felt as if part of her had just died. It was as if the flame of hope that had always burned within her—and not just for her brother—had been extinguished.

"Are you okay?" Lucas asked.

"No," she choked.

Lucas gently put his arm around her. "It's going to be all right," he soothed. "Benjamin is tough."

Zoey just shook her head, burying her face in her hands. "I feel so bad."

Lucas held her tightly. "He'll be okay, Zoey. I know he will. He hasn't lost anything."

Zoey leaned against Lucas, wishing she could believe him, trying to draw solace from the boy she loved. It felt so natural to be there with him, to be supported by his inner strength. But suddenly she remembered that she hadn't even seen or spoken to him in five days. She drew back.

"Lucas, what are you doing here?" she asked.

He swallowed. "I—uh—was waiting for you and your dad to get back, and then Nina showed up. She was a wreck."

"Waiting for me and my dad?" Zoey repeated.

He shook his head. "Waiting for *you*."

"Why?"

"Because I love you," he said simply.

She blinked, utterly bewildered. Hadn't he told her that he wanted nothing to do with her? "But—"

"Zoey, I spent all yesterday afternoon trying to track you down. And when I couldn't find you, I went home. I stayed up most of the night thinking of what I was going to say when I called you, but I couldn't come up with the right thing. So I just decided to come over this morning and talk to you in person. I knew that when I saw your face, I'd know what to say."

"And do you?" she breathed.

He smiled his sad smile, looking so beautiful in the winter sunlight with his blond hair hanging out from under his black wool cap. "No," he said. "I just know

169

that I love you. And I always will. Forever.'' He paused. "Do you still love me?"

Zoey nodded. She would never let him go again. And she knew that no matter what happened with Benjamin, or with Nina, or with Lara or Jake or *anyone*—if Lucas was by her side, she would have the strength to survive.

"Forever," she whispered.

Making Out:
Don't Tell Zoey

Book 13 in the explosive series about broken hearts, secrets, friendship, and of course, love.

At last **Zoey's** sure she loves **Lucas,** which leaves **Aaron** free for **Claire.** But then beautiful **Kate** moves into **Lucas's** house. Is **Zoey** about to discover how it feels to get hurt? The truth isn't always what it seems but...

Don't
tell
Zoey